FIVE CAT MAGIC

About the Author

Lisa Buddin is a qualified science teacher who has spent most of her career in the charity sector, raising awareness of human rights and environmental issues. Lisa is currently a tutor for mature students, and in 2018 began training to become a mindfulness teacher. Lisa lives in Buckinghamshire with her husband and two children.

About the Illustrator

Christine Jones is a freelance artist. Following a long career in Nursing, she achieved a lifetime ambition of continuing her art studies at University, where she gained a BA in Art and Design.

FIVE CAT
MAGIC

LISA BUDDIN

ILLUSTRATED BY CHRISTINE JONES

Matador
9 Priory Business Park,
Wistow Road, Kibworth Beauchamp,
Leicestershire. LE8 0RX
Tel: 0116 279 2299
Email: books@troubador.co.uk
Web: www.troubador.co.uk/matador
Twitter: @matadorbooks

ISBN 978 1789016 659

British Library Cataloguing in Publication Data.
A catalogue record for this book is available from the British Library.

Printed and bound in the UK by TJ International, Padstow, Cornwall
Typeset in 12pt Book Antiqua by Troubador Publishing Ltd, Leicester, UK

Matador is an imprint of Troubador Publishing Ltd

For James, Rebecca, Jessica & Ashley.
And for my skin & blisters, J & H.
With love, LB

Heartfelt thanks to Alex Hill, Christine Jones,
Matador & Nigel Peace.

To my dear friend Lindsay.

Sending you so much love on
your birthday.

You are always in my heart.

Lisa
x

2019

– CONTENTS –

– CHAPTER ONE –
GRANDMA'S PARTY

Jessica thought that her grandmother was as beautiful and elegant as a lily and had chosen to call her 'Lily' from when she was a very tiny girl. It was Grandma's special name and lilies were her favourite flowers. Jessica wondered if Lily would be at the party. She hoped so, because things were always more fun when Lily was around.

Jessica and her grandmother were very close. Lily was Jessica's best friend. They talked for hours and hours and always did lots of fun things together. Jessica especially liked to help her in the garden and Lily would spend hours telling Jessica about all the different plants and what the butterflies, bees and birds liked best. Grandma's garden was always full of birds of all different shapes and sizes and every type of insect imaginable.

At night time, hedgehogs, foxes and bats always came to visit. Grandma would talk to them as if they could understand what she was saying. Jessica would giggle thinking that her grandmother was being very silly.

"Why don't you play more with friends your own age?" Mum would often say to Jessica, "I think you spend too much time at Grandma's."

Jessica would just smile, laugh and say, "That's just the way it is," which would drive Mum mad!

The truth was, at ten years old, Jessica didn't have many friends her own age at school. The children at her school thought she was too quiet and, because she was smaller than the other children, they imagined that she was too young to join in with their 'grown up' conversations. Jessica didn't mind too much though. She liked to get on with her school work and, if she had to play with other children, she much preferred to spend time with her cousins exploring each other's gardens, making up stories and talking about all the exotic places they would visit when they were older. Her favourite thing though, above anything else, was to spend time with her grandmother.

Jessica had known that something wasn't right the day her Lily died. She had been thinking about her all day and could not get a song out of her head. It was her grandmother's favourite song and she always sang it whenever she needed cheering up, or when something important was happening. Jessica's father came to pick her up from school that day, which was very unusual, as it was always Mum who collected her. She knew as soon as she came out of school and saw him standing there that something was terribly wrong. Dad didn't say anything but he looked very sad. He led Jessica to the car, and once they were inside, taking her hand in his, he said in a quiet voice, "I'm so sorry Jessica, but something has happened to Grandma."

Jessica knew straight away.

"She died, didn't she," Jessica said.

"Yes," replied Dad.

"What happened?" asked Jessica.

"Well," said Dad, "we're not really sure, but it looks like she just fell asleep and didn't wake up. Your Mum rang her this morning but there was no reply, so she went over to see her. When she went inside she called out to Grandma but there was no answer. She went upstairs and found her lying on her bed. Mum said that she looked very peaceful."

"Is Mum very sad?" Jessica asked.

"Yes, she is," Dad replied, "but Grandma had a very good, long life and she can rest now."

Jessica had never been to a funeral before and wasn't sure what to expect or how she felt about it. What should she wear? Are you allowed to talk? Would she be expected to do anything? Would people cry?

Mum had told Jessica that they wanted to celebrate Grandma's life and to think of the day as a big party for all of Grandma's friends and family. Jessica was really looking forward to that part. Grandma had always enjoyed a good party. She loved to dance and tell jokes and eat lots of cake. Lily always managed to get most of her cake down her front, which made Jessica laugh. Jessica wondered if Lily would be at the party.

"Mum, can Grandma still hear me even though she's not here?" Jessica asked.

"What does your heart tell you?" said Mum.

"I've tried talking to her," Jessica said, "but she hasn't said anything back yet. I think she can hear me though."

"Grandma told me something once, just after Grandpa died," said Mum. "She told me that when a person is alive they are like a little hairy caterpillar and when they die, they turn into a beautiful butterfly and fly away so that you can't see them anymore. But just because you can't see them, it doesn't mean that they're not there, they've just changed form."

"That's nice," said Jessica.

"And the best bit is," said Mum, "that if you really pay attention and keep a look out, the person you love who has gone, will give you little signs to show you that they are still there with you and that they still love you."

"Maybe she's too busy meeting all her new butterfly friends!" said Jessica.

"Yes, that must be it" Mum said. "Now come on, you'd better get dressed otherwise we're going to be late."

Jessica put on her best dress and her favourite shoes. She wanted to look nice for Grandma. She also wore her silver locket that Grandma had given her as a baby. It had belonged to Grandma and when Jessica was old enough to understand, Grandma had explained that it was traditional to pass the locket on to the eldest female grandchild in the family. There was a beautiful diamond set in the middle of the front of the locket, surrounded by strange markings.

On the back were engraved the words:

Kindness, Peace, Hope, Freedom, Love

When the locket was open there was space for a picture in each of the two halves. On one side there was a picture of Grandma holding a cat and on the other there was an old, very faded black and white photograph of a little girl. Jessica had asked her grandmother who the little girl was.

Lily had just smiled and said, "Ah, you'll find out one day!"

Jessica liked to make up lots of stories and imagine who the little girl might have been. Perhaps it was Grandma when she was younger, but Jessica was not sure.

"Are you ready yet?" Mum called up the stairs. "We really need to go now, the car is here."

Before she left her bedroom, Jessica held her locket in both hands and whispered, "I know you can hear me Lily. I hope you are ok wherever you are and that you're having a good time. I miss you so much. Please watch over me and try to talk to me whenever you can. I hope you enjoy your party today. I love you."

Jessica decided that she did not really like funerals. There were too many people crying and the music they played in the church was very sad. It was not really the sort of music that Lily liked. The best bit though was when Mum read out a poem she had written for Grandma. It was lovely. Then it was time for the party.

Everyone went back to Grandma's house and it was nice to see so many of her friends there, even though Jessica did not know many of them. There was a lot of party food, cakes and sweets, it was a real feast. Grandma's favourite music was playing in the background and people were chatting and talking about the old times and telling funny stories they remembered about Grandma. Everyone had something nice to say about her and they all had fond memories.

One man was talking particularly loudly to a group of people. Jessica did not know him.

"Do you remember that cat she had?" he said. "It was the funniest little thing you know. It used to frighten me a bit. It would stare at me with these piercing blue eyes. I used to think it could look into my very soul and read my mind! I wonder what happened to it?"

"I think it ran away," said one lady.

"No, it got run over," said another.

"No no, that's rubbish," said a third, "she gave it away."

"Well, I don't know," said the man, "but I do remember that she had a couple of lovely cat ornaments. I wonder if I could see them again."

Jessica watched the man go over to Mum and speak to her briefly. Then Mum left the room and went upstairs. A few minutes later Mum returned, carrying two objects in her hands.

They were ornaments of two cats that had belonged to Lily. Jessica used to sit and play with them for hours in Grandma's house. They were very special and had been in their family for years. She thought they were beautiful and loved to look at them and hold them. One of the cats was carved from a beautiful piece of gold, which was perfectly smooth. The cat stood about 5 centimetres high. It was moulded into a seated position, its front legs straight and tall, with its head cocked slightly to the right. It was looking straight ahead and had the most wonderful yellow crystal kunzite eyes.

The second cat, Jessica's favourite, was made from stone, which was cool to the touch. It was very heavy, even though it was small enough to sit in the palm of her hand. It was grey in colour and was covered in a special sheen, which made it look like silk. It had been made so that it looked as though it was curled up, asleep, warming itself in front of an open fire.

After Jessica had finished playing with them, Grandma would always make sure that she put them back in the special display cabinet in her bedroom where she kept them. She would carry out the same ritual every time. She would kiss each of the cats, then place them in the cabinet. She would then take a key that she kept on a length of ribbon round her neck and lock the cabinet. All the time her lips would be moving as though she were saying a silent prayer.

When Jessica saw her mother with the cats, she felt a slight feeling of panic creeping up from the bottom of her stomach. She didn't know why, but she really did not like watching the small group of people around Mum looking at and touching the cats. Lily would not have liked it either.

Then as if out of nowhere, a tall, thin man moved closer to the group. He was very strange-looking to Jessica, she hadn't noticed him before.

He was looking at the cats in Mum's hands intensely and every now and then would lick his lips and cough slightly to clear his throat.

Then, in an even stranger voice, he said to Mum, "May I be so bold as to enquire at what price you would be willing to sell your, erherm, lovely prizes?"

Mum glanced up at him with a look of bewilderment.

"Well, I'm, I, I don't really, what I mean to say is, I'm not sure we want to sell – "

Her voice trailed off as though she just ran out of breath.

Jessica was starting to feel really scared now. They couldn't sell Grandma's cats, they just couldn't! She moved over to her mother and tugged her cardigan. Mum looked down at Jessica and for a moment still looked very bewildered and vacant. The look soon vanished and she turned back to the thin man and said, "I'm sorry but these cats are not for sale. They belong to my daughter Jessica now, my mother wanted her to have them."

"That is a pity," the thin man said, "I should very much have liked – no matter. There will be another time perhaps."

With that he turned and walked away.

"Jessica, can you take these back upstairs please," said Mum. "Here's the key to the cabinet. Grandma was still wearing it when she passed away."

Mum handed Jessica the cats and the ribbon with the key on it. She took them with relief.

"Did Grandma really want me to have them Mum?" Jessica asked.

"Yes," said Mum, "she told me a long time ago when you were born that should anything happen to her, the cats must go to you. She was very firm about it."

"Who was that man?" Jessica asked.

"I'm not sure." Mum said. "I've never seen him before. "Perhaps he was an old friend of your Grandma's."

"I doubt it." Jessica replied. "I didn't like him."

"He was a little strange." said Mum. "Never mind, he's gone now."

Jessica took the cats upstairs to Lily's bedroom and tried to copy her grandmother's ritual for putting them away as closely as she could. She didn't know what words Lily used to say, so she made up her own.

Jessica gave each cat a kiss on its head and said, "Beautiful cats, lovely cats, I will keep you safe and watch over you and never let anything bad happen to you. And I will never sell you, especially not to that nasty man and – "

"I wouldn't be so sure about that little girl."

Jessica was shocked to hear the hissing voice behind her and spun round in fright. Standing in the doorway of her grandmother's bedroom was the thin stranger. Jessica froze.

"Perhaps one day you will be only too happy to part with those feline thingsss," he hissed.

Jessica didn't know what to do so she let out the loudest, most ear-piercing scream her lungs could manage. It did the trick though. The thin man turned, ran down the stairs and out of the front door. Moments later Mum and Dad

12

came running up to the bedroom. Mum looked ghostly white.

"What happened?" Dad asked in dismay.

Jessica was crying now.

"It, it was that horrible man," she said, "he was here and he was trying to get the cats!"

Soon after, everyone left Grandma's house. Mum, Dad and Jessica were alone again. They decided to spend the night at Grandma's as it was quite a long drive back to their own house. Jessica was also very tired from the day and was still a little shaken up by what had happened. Before going to bed, Jessica checked on the cats one last time just to be sure that they were still safe.

Jessica did not sleep well that night. She kept waking up with a start and had a lot of bad dreams about the thin stranger and the cats and of scary things trying to get her. She also dreamt of her grandmother who kept trying to tell her something but Jessica could not hear her. She was glad when it was finally morning and she could get up.

Over the next few days, Mum and Dad were busy tidying Grandma's house, sorting out paperwork and trying to decide what to do with all her possessions. Jessica was busying herself in the garden, trying to clear some of the weeds that had taken root and were threatening to strangle Grandma's plants. She would miss Lily's house when it was sold.

Jessica wished that they could keep it so that she could be there whenever she wanted. She felt nearer to Grandma when she was in her home, as everything around her reminded her of Lily. She would look at all her things; her books, her paintings, her old photographs and she loved to wrap herself in Grandma's scarves and cardigans as they still smelt of her.

Jessica was woken from her thoughts by the sound of Mum's voice calling her from the upstairs window.

"Jess, can you come up for a minute, I've found something."

Jessica left her gardening and ran into the house and up the stairs. She found her mother sitting on Grandma's bed holding an envelope. Jessica sat beside her.

"I found this," Mum said as she handed the large brown envelope to Jessica. "It was in a box of old papers in Grandma's wardrobe."

Jessica looked at the envelope, which seemed worn and tattered around the corners. Jessica's name was written on the front in large letters in what was unmistakably Lily's handwriting.

Jessica sat there for a few moments just looking at the envelope.

"Well," said Mum impatiently, "are you going to open it then?"

"Yes, I will," replied Jessica, "but I think I would like to be by myself."

"Suit yourself," said Mum, "I'll be downstairs if you need me."

Jessica looked at the envelope for a few moments. For some reason she felt nervous and excited all at once. Then her curiosity got the better of her and she turned the envelope over and carefully opened it. There was a letter inside.

To my dearest, sweetest, darling girl, Jessica.
If you are reading this letter, it means that I am no longer with you…

– CHAPTER TWO –

THE LETTER

I hope that you are not too sad at my going. Please feel happy knowing that I am safe and well and that I will be with you, watching over you always.

I hope that your mother and father are well. Do not worry about my house, I trust that they will know what to do with it.

I want you to read what I am about to say very carefully. It is important that you learn what I write here and when you feel sure that you remember, you must destroy this letter so that it cannot be read by anyone else.

As has been the tradition in our family

for centuries, it is now my duty to pass this information on to you. As the eldest female grandchild, you are now the successor of a long line of females from our family who have been 'Guardians'. I will explain. Do not be afraid.

In the beginning, before our planet existed, before there was time, before there were people or animals, water or trees, there was only light. There was no war, no hunger, no death and no disease. The only beings which existed within the light called themselves 'the One' as they lived together in a state of perfect harmony, peace and happiness.

Then a time came when some of the beings of the One decided they would like to experience being on their own, as this had never been done before. The other light beings could not understand why they should wish to do this, but because they loved them very much, they agreed to let them go.

The One then created many different homes, which were called planets, for the beings to live on. The One also suggested that they choose a form or a body in which to live on the planets. Some chose to be animals, plants, and rocks as we know them. Some chose to take the form of things we can only imagine and some chose to take the form of human beings.

Some of the light beings then left the One and went to live in their new homes. For many, many years they were content with their new experiences and were happy to explore their new surroundings.

But before long they began to forget that they had once been part of the One, and as each generation went by, they grew more and more restless and unhappy. The One could see what was happening and out of love, tried to help them remember where they had come from. Some of the beings did remember in time and asked if they could return to the

One. But the others chose not to return and they gradually became bitter, sad and cruel.

After many years of harbouring these feelings, these beings took comfort from living in the darkness and they found pleasure in spreading terror, pain and desolation – it made them feel more powerful. Beings from all the planets began to live in fear of them and referred to them as the 'Shadow Beings'.

Soon, all of the planets were ruled by the darkness of the Shadow Beings. There was no more peace, no more beauty, no more joy and laughter, no more kindness, no more freedom, no more love. Instead there was cruelty, rage, despair, slavery and hatred. It was like being trapped in your deepest, darkest nightmare forever.

The One decided that something had to be done about the Shadow Beings and sent the most beloved parts of itself – the angels – to all the planets to restore balance. The angels battled with the Shadow Beings and their malicious followers for thousands of years. Many lives were lost.

At last the angels won through. The Shadow Beings were defeated and those that remained fled to planet Earth. The One knew that some of the Shadow Beings had escaped to Earth, but agreed to allow them to stay there, hidden and unable to cause harm in an invisible dark realm.

To ensure that the Shadow Beings would not threaten the planets again, the One appointed Gatekeepers of the dark realm to guard the Shadow Beings and help keep all life in balance. They took the form of five cats, each with a different magical power. The One then chose a very special being from Earth, a human, to be the Guardian of the cats. The Guardianship was handed down to the eldest female grandchild generation after generation and there was peace on all planets for many years.

For a long time, the Gatekeepers, the cats, were safe. They had been well hidden and were protected to prevent the Shadow Beings from finding them and escaping. But Jessica, the Shadow Beings have grown strong once more. A follower of the Shadow Beings was able to leave the dark realm and killed your four-times-great-grandmother. She was unable to tell anyone where the five cats were hidden before she died. The knowledge was lost.

Then, when I was a young girl, two of the cats were discovered and given to me to keep safe. It is vital that the other three cats are found before the Shadow Beings take them and escape from the dark realm. If this is allowed to happen, all beings will be in danger *and the planets will be plunged into darkness once more.*

Jessica, I am gone so it is up to you to be the Guardian now. I know it is a huge burden and responsibility but you are the only one who can do it. I have entrusted two of the cats to you and I know that you already love them and will protect them and keep them safe. During my time as the Guardian, I decided it was best to keep the cats as ornaments in my house to make them look ordinary in the hope that no one would notice them. But this is no longer safe Jessica, so you must do what you can to keep them hidden from the Shadow Beings.

Your challenge now is to find the other three cats. They only have true power and strength when all five are together. You will not be alone Jessica. There are many, many friends of the One who will help you, but it will not be easy and at times danger will be around every corner. You must take great care.

You will know when it is time for you to go in search of the other cats – you will be shown. Take heart! Know that I am always with you and that I will be there when you need me most.

Be safe my little one.

With love and light, Lily xxx

Jessica folded the letter up and laid it on her lap. She took a deep breath. Her mind was a whirl. She picked up the brown envelope and looked inside. At the bottom of it she could see something shiny and what looked like a large leaf. Jessica tipped the envelope upside down to empty it. There was the tiniest silver key, barely the length of her thumbnail and a large leaf-shaped piece of paper with writing on it. On the leaf were written the words, *You will know when to use this*, and a poem.

So five there are, five there'll be,
And I have travelled far
So come with me
Come wise cats hear my call
The forever darkness must never fall
Come sing with me and our hearts will soar
The dark realm will hide when it hears your roar

Jessica was overwhelmed. What did it all mean? There were a million and one different questions buzzing through her mind. Just then, Mum called up the stairs.

"Jess, are you ok? You've been up there ages."

Jessica was suddenly alert.

"I'm fine Mum," she said. "I'll be down in a minute."

Jessica picked up the envelope and placed the letter, key and leaf inside. Then she ran downstairs, past her bewildered-looking mother and out into the garden. Once outside, Jessica went and sat under her favourite tree and leant back so that the trunk was supporting her. She closed her eyes and just sat listening to the birds singing and feeling the warmth of the sun on her face.

Jessica wished that Lily was there. There were so many things she wanted to ask her. What were the Shadow Beings like? Where would she find the other three cats? Would she be in real danger? Should she tell Mum about the letter? Jessica felt a bit helpless and very, very small. A single tear ran down her face.

Just at that moment Jessica heard a bird call. It sounded very close by and made her open her eyes to look. Right in front of her, about an arm's length away was a tiny robin redbreast.

It was looking at her with its beady black eyes, head cocked to the side and its chest all puffed up. The little bird made Jessica laugh.

"Hello, what's your name?" she asked.

The bird looked at her for a while longer then turned and flew away.

"Bye then," Jessica said. "Didn't you want to stay any longer?"

Jessica was just about to close her eyes again when she saw the robin sitting on the fence in front of her. It looked like it had something in its mouth.

"What have you got there?" Jessica asked the bird.

Then the robin flew straight over to her, dropped its passenger into her lap and flew away again. Jessica was fascinated. She looked down to see what it was the bird had left for her.

At first, she felt slightly disgusted when she realised that it was a tiny, hairy green caterpillar. She was just about to flick it off her lap when she remembered what her mother had told her. Jessica very gently picked the creature up between her thumb and forefinger and placed it on the palm of her hand.

"Hello there Mr Caterpillar," she said. "Did Lily send you to make me feel better?"

Jessica stood up and carried the caterpillar over to a small green bush that she thought would look tasty to a caterpillar. She carefully placed her furry friend onto a leaf and said, "I hope you turn into a beautiful butterfly one day."

When Jessica sat down under her tree again she felt much better and not so alone. She decided to read Grandma's letter once more to make sure that she remembered everything that had been said.

When she had finished reading she went back into the house to speak to her mother.

"Mum. I've read Grandma's letter. She only wanted me to read it and she told me that I should destroy it to make sure no one else saw it. Will you help me? I think we should burn it."

"Ok," said Mum, "but don't you think that's a bit extreme? Are you sure you want to burn it?"

"Yes, I am," replied Jessica. "Grandma was very clear that it needed to be destroyed once I had read it."

"Right," said Mum, "well, we had better get right to it then. Trust Grandma to be so secretive! She had a very vivid imagination my mother."

Mum and Jessica went back out to the garden and Jessica placed the letter in the special metal bin that Grandma used to have bonfires. Then Mum threw some dry leaves on top of it and lit a match.

"Are you sure you want to do this?" Mum asked again.

"Yes, it needs to be done," said Jessica.

With that, Mum placed the lighted match on top of the leaves and they watched as the fire took hold, flames licking their way round the pieces of paper. Mum went back into the house, but Jessica just stood watching the fire, transfixed by the beautiful colours.

She wasn't sure, but she thought she could see little silver stars jumping up out of the flames every so often. Jessica stayed watching the small fire until she was sure every last piece of the letter had burned. Satisfied that the letter had gone, Jessica went back into the house, clutching the brown envelope tightly.

- CHAPTER THREE -

MR WICKER

Life carried on as normal for Jessica and her family. Time went by and before they knew it, almost a year had passed since Lily's funeral. Jessica still missed her grandmother terribly, but as is often the case, she felt a little better and a little less sad as each day went by.

When Jessica was alone, she would still think about Lily's letter and the story of the Shadow Beings and the cats. She had believed in the story so much when she first read about it, it had seemed so real. But now she was not so sure. To her it seemed as though a long time had gone by. Without Lily around to tell her fantastic stories of other worlds, magical people and strange, wonderful creatures, she found it more difficult to believe. Plus, she was a year older now and preparing to go to her new secondary school; she felt a bit silly to still believe in such things. Jessica's life seemed more ordinary now that Lily was not around.

Grandma's house had also been sold and Jessica felt as though her connection to Lily had been broken. She was very upset the day Dad told her that the house had gone. But at least she still had the two cats. Jessica had got into the habit of carrying the cats, the key and the poem with her wherever she went. She kept them in a small velvet bag attached to a long ribbon, which she wore around her neck. Even though she was not sure if she believed in the Shadow Beings, the memory of the thin stranger at Lily's party had stayed with her. She did not want to leave the cats alone.

The summer holidays came and went again in a flash and before she knew it, Jessica had started at her new school. It was quite frightening to begin with as it was so much bigger than her old school and she was now the youngest there. Some of the teachers were quite scary too. But she made some new friends quickly, worked hard and settled in very well.

Then one afternoon Jessica was in a classroom, sitting at her desk waiting for her teacher to arrive to begin the lesson. It was unusual for the teacher to be late and the class had started to get restless and begun to chatter.

No one noticed when the door opened and someone walked in and sat behind the teacher's desk at the front of the class. Jessica was in full flow, telling a girl next to her about her weekend, when she felt the hairs on the back of her neck stand up. She stopped talking in the middle of her sentence.

"Jess, carry on, what were you saying?" said the girl impatiently.

Jessica could not speak. She was staring at the front of the classroom at the person sitting behind the teacher's desk. All conversations in the room had stopped and everyone was looking at the person who had silently entered the room.

"Who's that?" whispered the girl.

Jessica did not reply.

The person stood up and started to walk down the rows of desks looking at each pupil as he went. The room was silent and it felt as though everyone was holding their breath. When the man got to Jessica's desk he stopped and looked at her for what felt like forever. Jessica felt sick. Then the man went back to the desk at the front of the room.

"My name is Mr Wicker," said the man. He paused as if waiting for someone to challenge him. "Unfortunately, your teacher Miss Shepherd has been taken ill. I have been asked to take her class. I trust that you will, erherm, be gracious enough to allow me to teach you – "

Jessica did not hear anything else he said. She had gone into shock. She had not been sure until he had cleared his throat. Now she was convinced. It was the thin stranger from her grandmother's funeral! Jessica didn't know what to do. She could not believe her eyes.

The whole lesson was a blur and Jessica could not remember anything that had been said. She just recalled having a sick feeling in her stomach the whole time. As soon as the lesson was over and it was time to go, Jessica grabbed her bag and made for the door. She froze when she felt a bony finger tap her on the shoulder.

"I would very much like for you to stay behind for a few moments pleassse."

It was Mr Wicker, if that was his real name.

Jessica was terrified.

"I, I, h-have to go," she stammered.

A shiver ran down her back as though someone had trickled an ice cube along her spine.

"It will not take long," Mr Wicker replied.

Jessica watched in dismay as all her

classmates left one by one. She saw the girl she had been sitting next to and looked at her with imploring eyes, trying to send her a silent message that she needed help.

"I'll see you in the next lesson," the girl said as she left the room.

When they were alone, Mr Wicker invited Jessica to sit down and then he began to talk.

"I have been led to believe that your teacher, Miss Shepherd is very ill indeed. It could be quite some time before she is well enough to return to school. In fact," he said, moving closer to Jessica, "she may not be well enough to come back at all. So I will be here indefinitely. I do hope that you will enjoy my lessons. I am sure you will come to trust me in time."

Jessica was not really paying attention to what he was saying; she was mesmerized by the way the man's tongue kept flicking out.

Then, from somewhere deep inside her, Jessica plucked up the courage to speak to the man.

"I know who you are," she said. "You were at my Grandma's house."

The man seemed taken aback by the way Jessica had spoken so forcefully, she had almost shouted at him.

"I think you are mistaken little girl," he said. "I have never met you before and I was certainly not at your grandmother's funeral."

"I didn't say you were at her funeral," replied Jessica coldly.

The man looked nervous and his tongue flicked out more and more. Just then the door of the classroom opened and a mass of students flooded through, arriving for the next lesson.

Jessica took the opportunity to stand up and head for the door. As she walked through she glanced over her shoulder to see if the man was following her. He was standing where she had left him but his eyes were still fixed on her. Jessica shot out of the door with a shudder.

The rest of the afternoon passed without incident but Jessica was left feeling very shaken. The last place she expected to see the thin stranger again was at her school!

Jessica felt relieved when it was the end of the day and she could go home. Thoughts of Mr Wicker and what he had said ran through her mind as she walked home. That night she was very quiet and did not eat much of her dinner.

"Are you feeling ok?" asked Mum. "You look a little pale."

"I feel a bit sick Mum," replied Jessica, "maybe I shouldn't go to school tomorrow."

"Ah, that old one," joked Mum. "Haven't you got a test tomorrow? Maybe you should have an early night, get some rest. I'm sure you'll feel much better in the morning."

For some reason Jessica did not want to tell her mother about Mr Wicker. She did not want to worry her Mum and now that she was in the safety of her home, she wondered if she had imagined that it was the same man.

As she sat in her bedroom her thoughts turned to Lily. Jessica lifted each of the cats out of the velvet bag and held one in each hand, a lovely warm feeling flowed over her. She still loved the cats very much and they reminded her of Lily.

"I wish you were here Lily," Jessica sighed to herself. "You'd know what to do about Mr Wicker. I wonder if he is the same person who was in your house? Is he anything to do with the Shadow Beings? And why did he keep looking at my bag? It was as if he knew the cats were inside. I don't know, it's all very confusing."

That night, Jessica asked Lily to arrange for the angels to watch over her and keep her safe. She slept with the cats under her pillow, one hand in constant contact with them.

Jessica had a very strange dream that night. She was climbing some stone stairs that were built into the side of an enormous rock. But however many steps she climbed she couldn't seem to get any nearer to the top. She was getting very tired and felt as though she were carrying a heavy weight. She was exhausted and decided to stop and sit on one of the steps to get her breath back. She looked down, and for a moment, she thought she could just make out the word *Soon* etched in the dust. She blinked and looked again but the word had gone. Then she looked up in the sky and saw a whole flock of birds flying above.

The birds were flying in a strange formation and again, just for a second, Jessica was sure that the birds had formed a position to spell out the words *Get Ready*.

Jessica woke with a start and whilst she was still in that moment between sleep and wakefulness, she was sure she heard a little voice say, "It's time."

Jessica looked much better in the morning and although she told Mum that she felt unwell, Mum insisted that she went into school.

"I really think you should go in Jess," Mum said. "If you still feel poorly at lunchtime ask someone in the school office to ring me at work and I'll come and get you."

Reluctantly, Jessica got ready and set off for school. It was not very far to walk, but she took her time and walked very slowly. She really did not want to go in. She had started to get that nervous feeling in her stomach when she thought about having to face Mr Wicker again. The dream from the night before also made her a little apprehensive and she wondered what it meant.

Just then she became aware of a car pulling up next to her. She ignored it and carried on walking, quickening her pace slightly. She heard the car door open and then the voice.

"Erherm, Jessica, stop there."

Jessica knew who it was. She froze but could not help turning her head. It was Mr Wicker.

"You are going to be late for school," he said. "I will drive you the rest of the way. Get in the car."

Jessica panicked. She didn't know what to do. She felt really scared and the last thing she wanted to do was to get in the car with him.

A voice inside her head shouted, *Run!*

Jessica ran blindly up the road. She didn't even know where she was going, she just knew she had to get away from Mr Wicker. She heard the man shout behind her, he sounded angry. Jessica ran and ran. She could see a row of small shops ahead of her on the other side of the road. She would be safe there. If she could just get to the shops she could get away from him and get help. Jessica stepped into the road to run across, then…

…everything froze. It was as though the whole world just stopped. Jessica thought she was still running but she felt as though her body was in treacle and all her movements were very slow. Then she just stopped. She looked around in amazement.

There was no movement at all. The cars on the road had stopped; the people inside were still like statues; the birds in the sky were frozen as they flew; there was no wind in the trees; people on the street had stopped, their walking interrupted, feet hanging in the air waiting to make contact with the ground again. It was like someone had pressed pause. It was only Jessica who could still move.

Then, as Jessica looked on, everything around her began to wobble. It was like the scene in front of her had become a huge jelly on a plate. She realised that she could not see any colours; everything was grey. Then there was a flash of bright white light that hurt her eyes with its intensity and made her close them. Shielding her eyes with her hand, Jessica slowly looked around and was awestruck by what she saw.

Just then a beautiful girl came running towards Jessica, her long golden hair flowing behind her. She looked a few years older than Jessica.

"Quick!" she shouted. "You must come with me. We have to hide!"

Before Jessica had time to respond, the girl grabbed her by the hand and they both started to run. It felt like they were running on air and they were going very fast.

"We must get to lower ground," shouted the girl.

With that, they ran towards an enormous tree that looked as though it had part of its trunk

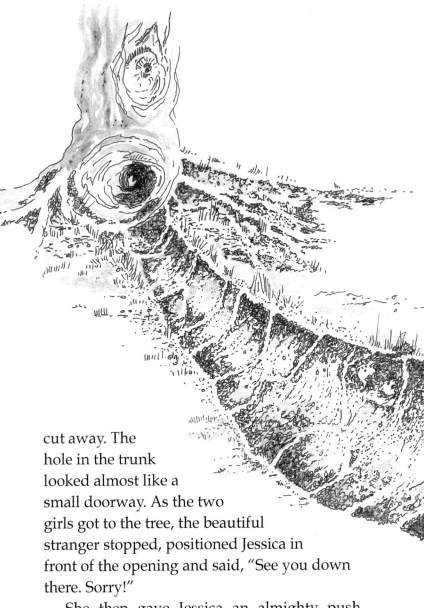

cut away. The
hole in the trunk
looked almost like a
small doorway. As the two
girls got to the tree, the beautiful
stranger stopped, positioned Jessica in
front of the opening and said, "See you down
there. Sorry!"

She then gave Jessica an almighty push,
which sent her flying through the opening of
the tree.

Down, down, down she fell. It felt as though she were in a tunnel on a huge slide going down and round, round and down. She could hear someone screaming, then realised she was making the noise. When she stopped she discovered that she actually felt quite safe and although the tunnel was dark, it was lit slightly by tiny little lights that surrounded her on all sides.

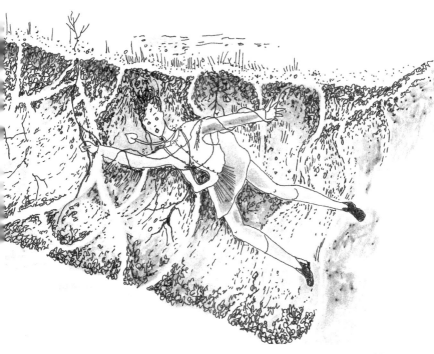

At last she came to an abrupt stop at what she assumed was the bottom. The girl landed beside her with a bump.

"Sorry about that," the girl said through a laughing smile, "but we had to get down here quick."

"Who are you?" Jessica enquired with an air of wonderment in her voice.

"My name is Rebecca," the girl replied. "Welcome to my home."

- CHAPTER FOUR -

TEA TIME

Jessica did not have time to ask the girl any further questions. Rebecca jumped up and in a loud whisper said, "Come on! They might still be following us. We have to get going."

"Who are *they*?" asked Jessica.

"No time now," said Rebecca. "I'll explain everything soon."

Before Jessica could say anything else, Rebecca took off, running down a dark passageway just in front of them. Not wanting to be left alone, Jessica got up, shook the dust from her clothes and ran after Rebecca shouting, "Wait for me!"

The passageway was so dark that Jessica could barely see her hand in front of her face. She could just make out Rebecca's silhouette in the gloom. Her long hair seemed to shimmer and sparkle slightly as she ran and Jessica found it comforting in the darkness.

The passageway was full of twists and turns and at one point the way seemed to be blocked by a mass of tree roots which were growing down through the roof of the passageway into the ground below. Rebecca and Jessica picked their way carefully through the roots. Jessica thought that she could actually see the roots moving slightly as they passed as if to allow them to get through, but she decided it was her eyes playing tricks on her.

Once the girls were through the tree roots, the passageway narrowed so much that they had to crouch down very small so as not to bump their heads. All the time they were in the passageway, Jessica had the distinct feeling that they were not alone. Although she could not see much around her, she fancied that she could sense tiny eyes watching them and at one point she thought she could hear whispers and muffled laughter.

Just as Jessica's back was starting to hurt from being hunched over, Rebecca stopped suddenly.

"Right, here we are," she exclaimed.

"Where?" Jessica asked, peering around her. "There's nothing here. It's all just tunnel still."

"Silly. Can't you see the door?" Rebecca asked.

"What door? There's no door here," said Jessica impatiently.

"Well, if there's no door, how do you think I can do this?" replied Rebecca.

With that she walked towards the rocky side of the passageway and vanished.

"Hey, where did you go?" shouted Jessica. "Don't leave me here."

Jessica almost jumped out of her skin as a head suddenly appeared out of the rocks. It was Rebecca.

"Come on," she said, "you don't want to get left behind!"

With that an arm appeared and grabbed Jessica, pulling her towards the rocks. Jessica shrieked as she shut her eyes tightly and braced herself, waiting for her head to bump on the side of the tunnel. But it never happened.

Instead she could feel a slight breeze on her face, warmth on her skin and she could just make out the most wonderful smell. Jessica opened her eyes slowly and blinked several times until she got used to the bright light. Jessica let out a tiny gasp. She was in the most beautiful place she had ever seen.

As Jessica looked around she realised that she was standing at the edge of a forest. Right behind her were the most enormous, tall, green trees. They appeared to reach for miles into the sky, as she could not see the tops. She could hear birdsong all around her and could just make out the shapes of tiny birds hopping from branch to branch in the huge trees. In front of Jessica was a small semi-circular bay, which had the purest white, sparkling sand Jessica had ever seen. The sea was gently lapping at the shore and Jessica thought she could hear the faint sound of harps playing. In the distance she could see snow-capped mountains.

"Where are we?" Jessica asked in a whisper.

She had not realised until then that she had been holding her breath.

"New Zealand," replied Rebecca, then she laughed. "Only joking. We're not really in New Zealand, although it is a lot like this. It doesn't have a name, it's just the place where I live," she said. "Well, most of the time anyway. Come on, let's go and talk somewhere else."

The two girls walked along the beach and Jessica stopped just long enough to take her shoes off. She wanted to feel the sand between her toes and longed to go for a paddle in the sea.

As if reading her mind, Rebecca said, "I wouldn't go in there just yet. The mermaids are out and they might just fancy you as a new sister!"

"The mermaids!" Jessica said in surprise. "Where on earth are we?"

"All will be revealed soon. Are you always this impatient?" said Rebecca laughing.

"Well, I'm sorry," replied Jessica, "but it's not every day you get pushed inside a tree, fall into a tunnel, walk through rocks and find yourself in a strange land surrounded by mermaids!"

"Well, that depends on who you talk to," said Rebecca with a wry smile on her face.

The two girls made their way carefully through the forest until they reached a small clearing. A tiny stream trickled alongside them and as Jessica followed the flow of water with her eyes she noticed that it ran straight past a small log cabin. She was still walking barefoot and became aware of the fact that the grass beneath her feet felt like velvet. By the side of the stream were many flowers of all different shapes, sizes and colours and it appeared as though they were dancing and swaying in the slight breeze.

"Here we are," Rebecca said.

"There's that smell again," Jessica said, interrupting the stillness.

"Ah, that'll be Leo cooking. You're in for a treat!" said Rebecca as she walked up to the entrance of the cabin.

The door of the small log house opened, as if by itself. Rebecca walked in and motioned for Jessica to follow her.

"Uugh?" grunted Jessica. "Sorry," she said, "I didn't mean to sound rude, it's just that, well, where is everything?"

Jessica was surprised. There was absolutely nothing inside the cabin. It had a roof, walls, windows and a floor, but not one piece of furniture, curtains or a plate, nothing.

"Well, well, well," said a gruff voice, "you've

taken your time haven't you. I was getting all in a fluster and the food is half ruined and my poor belly was a rumbling and everything."

Jessica spun round to see where the voice was coming from. Standing just inside the doorway was a peacock. Its head was bent slightly to one side and it was holding its wings in such a way as to make it look like it had feathery hands on its hips. Jessica wondered if she was hearing things. Then she let out a small chuckle of surprise as the peacock had a small, neat apron tied around its middle.

"Well, well, well. I don't know. You take your time and then you gets the giggles. I don't think much of your friend's manners B."

"Oh, I'm sorry," said Jessica, "I didn't mean to laugh. It's just that I've never heard an animal talk before or seen one wearing an apron!"

"An animal! An animal she says!" replied the peacock indignantly. "Well, well, well, bless my poor feathers. Who are you calling an animal? And what do you mean, you've never heard an *animal* talk before, eh missy? I don't know, you hoomans."

"Oh, Leo, come on now," said Rebecca, "don't be hard on her, this is all new. Or at least she has forgotten that she once knew about such things. So, it is up to us to be kind and help her to remember isn't it Leo?"

"Umph. Well, best she minds her manners," replied Leo as he bustled past them and into the room, his long, beautiful peacock tail swishing from side to side as he walked. "Has the hooman got a name?" Leo asked, looking down his beak at Jessica.

"The HUman's name is Jessica," said Rebecca with a raised eyebrow, "and I want you to be nice Leo, she is a special friend."

"Well then, you had better take a seat and we'll get the food all served up," said the peacock.

Jessica looked around her.

"Erm, I don't mean to sound rude," she said, "but where should I sit? There aren't any chairs."

"No chairs, no chairs," said Leo. "Where did you find this one B?"

"Leo!" replied Rebecca with a friendly warning tone in her voice.

"Alright, keep your feathers on. There are plenty of chairs to sit on. In fact, there are hundreds, thousands even," the peacock chuckled. "All you gotta do is think of one. Yes, just close your eyes and think of what chair you'd like to sit on. You gotta picture it good though, what it looks like, what it's made of, what it feels like, how big it is, that sort of thing. Go on, try it."

Jessica closed her eyes and instantly had a picture in her mind of a chair. It was a familiar chair, one she had sat on many, many times before. It was her grandmother's favourite chair and the one she used to sit on with Jessica on her lap when she told her a story. The memory made Jessica feel all warm and lovely inside. Then she opened her eyes.

To her astonishment, the very chair she had been thinking of was right in front of her. She could not believe it. It looked exactly like Grandma's chair. Jessica moved closer and put her nose close to it.

"Hey, it even smells like Grandma's chair!" she said in amazement.

"Well of course it smells like her chair. It is her chair!" said Leo. "Go on, sit down then, try it out."

Jessica cautiously sat down on the chair. It really was Grandma's chair!

"Right, time for eats," said Leo.

As Jessica sat in her chair looking at the peacock she could not believe what she was seeing. Right in front of her very eyes different objects were rapidly appearing out of thin air. First another chair, a large, round, yellow one with an enormous squashy cushion for Rebecca. Then a small, plain wooden stool for Leo, a table, plates, cups, knives and forks.

As Jessica looked around her, the whole cabin began to fill with different bits and pieces of furniture and other items you would expect to find in a home.

"What would you like to eat Jess?" asked Rebecca. "You can have anything you like. Close your eyes like before and imagine what it is you would most love to eat right now."

Jessica closed her eyes and thought. She was actually very hungry and imagined a huge plate of fish fingers and peas. Then pickled onions popped into her head, followed by ice cream, jam tarts and grapes. When she opened her eyes,

PICKLED ONIONS

there in front of her was a whole plate of fish fingers, a bowl of peas, an enormous jar of pickled onions, a platter of jam tarts and in the middle of the table was a large sculpture of a peacock made from chocolate ice cream!

Jessica laughed out loud.

"I can't believe it," she said. "That's exactly what I was thinking of! But hang on, I thought about grapes as well."

"You don't look very far do you," said Leo. "They're up there."

The peacock pointed upwards with his wing. Part of the roof of the cabin was missing and growing through the gap, along the rafters was a grape vine, heavy with real bunches of grapes.

Very soon the whole table was laden with all sorts of food and Jessica, Rebecca and Leo were happily tucking into their feast.

When they were full, Leo stood up.

"Well, I'll let you two get to business," he said. "You must have a lot of questions to ask young lady. B can tell you all about it. That's it, that's it. I'll get on with the clearing up. You two talk now."

The peacock began clearing the plates from the table, muttering to himself all the while.

"You probably do have a lot of questions," said Rebecca, "but I think that it's best for me to tell you a few things first and then you can ask me afterwards."

Jessica nodded in agreement and relaxed back into her chair with a steaming mug of hot chocolate and marshmallows that had just appeared on the table.

- CHAPTER FIVE -

THE INVISIBLE WORLD

Rebecca began her story.

"We are now in a place that some call the *Invisible World.* It is the place that many have a feeling exists but are not sure, as it cannot be seen. It is the place you go to in your dreams".

Rebecca went on to describe the Invisible Word as the place where you get your most fantastic ideas from. The place that causes you to have that wonderful feeling of excitement and happiness in the pit of your belly. She explained that it is the home of fairies, gnomes, dragons and mermaids, all the fantastical creatures and places that you thought were just made up in stories. It is the place where dreams can come true and where anything is possible. It is that space in between what some would call reality and another place. That wondrous place that you know in your heart exists and is your true home, but you have never seen. The place where some humans believe you go to when your physical body dies.

"As wonderful and beautiful as the Invisible World is Jessica, there is another side to it."

At this point Jessica thought she saw Rebecca shudder slightly before she continued.

"I know you have heard of the dark realm."

"Yes, yes, I have heard of it," Jessica said excitedly, "my grandmother told me about it in her letter."

"Shush!" warned Rebecca as her voice dropped to a whisper. "Do not speak of your grandmother's letter just yet. Even here, *they* may be listening."

Rebecca continued. "The dark realm exists here within the Invisible World and it is the stuff of nightmares. It is home to the loathsome Shadow Beings. The dark realm has been well guarded for thousands of years to prevent the Shadow Beings from escaping and wreaking havoc once more, like before—"

Rebecca's voice trailed off and she had a distant, haunted look in her eyes.

"Rebecca," Jessica called and gently touched the girl's arm.

Rebecca came back to herself.

"I'm sorry," she said, "where was I? Oh yes – well guarded. But the guardianship has been weakened Jessica and with the loss of three of the Gatekeepers, the Shadow Beings have been able to escape from the dark realm bit by bit and to cause chaos once more. There is evidence of it all over your world now. It has also been said that the Shadow Beings have captured one of the Gatekeepers, but I do not know if this is true." Rebecca paused, let out a long sigh and suddenly looked very old and tired as though she were carrying a very heavy weight. She continued, "That is why you have been sent for Jessica. As the Guardian of the Gatekeepers it is up to you to find them and bring all five together once more to restore order."

"With our help of course," a voice said.

Jessica looked up. She recognised the voice instantly.

"Lily!" she shouted.

Jessica jumped from her chair and ran, laughing into the open arms of her grandmother.

"But how, why, how is it possible, how can it be?" Jessica asked through sobs of joy, holding her grandmother tightly. "I don't understand," she sobbed.

"All things are possible in the Invisible World," chirped Leo, coming back to join the trio. "It's a bit like the chair and the food," he said. "You wanted it and you imagined it, so there it was. Did you imagine your grandmother being here and helping you?"

"Well, yes, I suppose I did," replied Jessica.

"There you go then," said the peacock, "here she is."

"I cannot stay with you for long," said Lily. "There are many things to arrange and put in place."

"There's so much to take in," Jessica said. "Is it all real? I feel as though I were in a dream. A wonderful dream, now that you are here Lily."

Jessica hugged her grandmother once more. "I've missed you so much," she said. "Are you well? You look well. Did it hurt when you died?" Jessica enquired.

Lily laughed.

"Oh, Jess, you are a funny one. Yes, I am quite well, and no, it didn't hurt when I died! I have been here in the Invisible World getting things ready and waiting for you to come. Now little one, listen carefully as I must leave you again for the time being. I have a message for you."

Lily motioned for Jessica to sit down whilst they talked.

"It is rumoured that one of the Gatekeepers has been seen not far from here. But you must hurry. The agents of the Shadow Beings also have this information and they will be on their way to try to capture the cat themselves. All I know is that the cat was last seen two days ago at the Full Moon Inn. Now I must leave you."

"Wait!" shouted Jessica in dismay. "Will I see you again?"

Lily turned, smiled and touched Jessica gently on the cheek.

"I'm never far away. If you really need me I will come. But do not fear little one, you have lots of friends here." She turned to Rebecca. "Do not forget to hide the Gatekeepers, they must not be found."

In the next second Lily was gone.

Jessica sank back in her chair.

"I don't believe it," she said, as if to herself. "Did I really just see Lily? It is all so strange."

"I know it is difficult for you to understand," said Rebecca reassuringly, "but you will get used to it. You have to get used to it Jess. We need you and you are here now. Just remember to try and keep an open mind."

Rebecca put her hand on Jessica's shoulder.

"Come now," she said, "there is much to be done. We should leave soon. They probably know that you are here by now so we must go. But first – the other Gatekeepers – do you have them?"

"The Gatekeepers?" enquired Jessica.

"Yes, the two cats – do you have them with you?" asked Rebecca.

"Oh, of course! I keep them with me all the time," replied Jessica. "I have them here in my bag—"

Jessica put her hand to her chest.

"Oh no, where is the bag? It was around my neck. The cats are in the bag but it's gone!" Jessica cried in dismay.

"Perhaps you dropped it on the way here," said Rebecca looking perplexed. "Or maybe it came off in the tunnel on your way down. We'll have to re-trace our steps and find it before *they* do."

"I'm so sorry," said Jessica. "I don't go anywhere without them, I don't know how I could have lost them and I've only just got here!"

"Come now," replied Rebecca, "do not lose heart, we will find them!"

She turned to the peacock.

"Leo, you know what to do once we have left?"

"Of course, of course," replied Leo, "you just leave it to me B."

"Thank you, my friend," said Rebecca. "Let's go Jess."

Rebecca took her by the hand and as the two girls walked out of the door Jessica said, "Bye Leo, very nice to meet you."

"Likewise, young lady, likewise," replied the peacock. "You take very good care now. Hopefully I'll see you again very soon," he added with a tinge of sadness in his voice.

The girls had barely walked more than ten paces when Jessica decided to turn and take one last look at the mysterious cabin. But the house was no longer to be seen.

"It's gone!" cried Jessica.

"Of course," laughed Rebecca, "we can't be too careful. I don't want just anybody going into my home."

"I shouldn't really be surprised by now," Jessica replied with a smile, her spirits lifting once more.

The girls re-traced their steps as Rebecca had suggested. Back through the clearing, across the sandy beach and past the sea until they got to the edge of the forest where they had started.

"Mmmm," mused Rebecca, "the only problem is, the entrance to the tunnel is never in the same place twice. So, in fact, it could be anywhere amongst the trees."

Jessica could feel herself becoming disheartened once again. Just then, they heard the sound of a dog barking very close by, then a whistle.

"Quick!" whispered Rebecca. "We need to hide!"

The girls ran into the forest and crouched down low behind a huge fern, trying to remain unseen. Then they heard a voice very near to them say, "Come out, come out wherever you are."

Jessica's blood froze. She was terrified. In the next second, they heard the sound of something coming very quickly towards them through the undergrowth. Jessica wanted to scream. They saw the black shiny nose first, then it was on them.

"Hey, stop that, get off!" Jessica yelled as the large black dog pinned her to the ground and licked her face.

"It's Tom!" shouted Rebecca with delight.

"I don't care who it is, just make this dog stop licking me!" Jessica shouted.

They heard the whistle again and the dog left as quickly as he had arrived. Rebecca stood up and called, "James, is that you?"

"At your service," a voice behind them replied.

The girls turned around to see a man standing behind them with the black dog by his side.

"James, James!" Rebecca cried with excitement as she rushed over to the man and threw her arms around him.

"Well, I should go away more often if that's the sort of welcome back I get!" he said laughing.

Rebecca punched him playfully on the arm.

"I don't think so," she said, "you've already been gone for at least twenty-two years!"

"Ah come now," he replied, "don't exaggerate, it's only been about eighteen! So who's your friend?" his attention now turned to Jessica.

"James, I would like you to meet Jessica," said Rebecca.

"Very pleased to meet you," James said as he extended his hand toward Jessica. "This is my very good friend Tom," he said, motioning towards the dog, which barked as if in response.

"I think I have something that belongs to you," said James as he held the small velvet bag out towards Jessica.

"Oh, you found it!" Jessica exclaimed. "Thank you so much. I thought I had lost it and we were just coming back to look for it."

Jessica took the bag from James and was about to place it round her neck when she dropped it to the floor with a shriek. The bag was wriggling. James laughed and bent down next to the bag. As he opened it, two little heads popped out.

"Phew," said one of the heads, "it was getting a little hot in there."

"I know," said the other head, "no ventilation in this thing, you could suffocate in here."

At that, the bodies of the heads emerged from the bag and as they began to grow in size, Jessica could see that they were in fact two real cats. One had a beautiful golden coat, the other was silky and light grey in colour.

"Jessica!" the cats said in unison and immediately rushed to the girl's side, purring loudly and rubbing their faces against her legs.

"Cats?" Jessica said in disbelief. "Is it you? But, but you're real!"

"Of course we're real," said the gold cat.

"We've always been real," said the grey cat, "we've just had to pretend to be like statues."

The cat pulled a face and suddenly stood very still.

"Yes, and it's not good for the joints being in one position the whole time," said the gold cat.

"It feels so good to be able to move again," said the grey cat as she started to leap in the air. "And I'm so hungry, what's for dinner?"

"Don't get too excited," said James, "we can't have you running around drawing attention to yourselves, it's not safe."

"We know," groaned the cats in unison, "but it's so nice. Can we stay like this a bit longer, please, please, please!"

"Well, just for the moment," replied James, "but you have to promise to change back when we ask you."

"You got it," said the cats.

"Let's go somewhere slightly safer," said James. "Follow me."

James and Tom the dog led the way with Jessica and Rebecca following. The cats were behind them, enjoying their freedom, rolling and frolicking in the long grass as they went.

- CHAPTER SIX -

THE CEREMONY

They followed James and Tom for quite some time through the forest, which seemed to get denser and more difficult to walk through with each step. Just when Jessica thought her legs could not keep going, James stopped and listened. They could just make out the faint sound of flowing water.

"Nearly there," James said, "not far now."

At last they came to the source of the sound – a magnificent waterfall in the heart of the forest. Jessica thought it was the most beautiful thing she had ever seen. The water flowed from high above their heads and cascaded down the rock face into a deep blue pool below. The pool was surrounded on all sides by large flat boulders and in between each of the boulders were strange, exotic plants of a kind Jessica had never seen before.

"Right, follow me," James said, "but watch your step, it can get very slippery."

Jessica watched as James and Tom gracefully stepped across the boulders and then seemed to disappear through the waterfall.

"Erm, excuse me," said the grey cat, "but you don't want *us* to go in there do you?"

"You're not being a scaredy cat are you?" joked Rebecca.

"I'm with her," said the gold cat, "I'm not getting my fur wet for anyone!"

Just then, Tom the dog came bounding back out onto the boulders and stood there barking at them as if to say, "Come on! What's the hold up?"

"Well, you'll just have to get back in the bag and I'll carry you," said Jessica.

The cats both looked at each other then turned their backs and huddled together. Jessica could hear them muttering to each other and it sounded as though they were having an argument.

"Well, ok," said the gold cat, "we'll get back in the bag, but if we get wet, you owe us a big juicy fish, each!"

Jessica placed the open bag on the ground. Before her very eyes, the cats began to reduce in size and reluctantly climbed inside the bag, then they all set off across the boulders. As they reached the gushing water, Rebecca motioned for Jessica to go first. She held her breath and closed her eyes as she walked into the falls. When Jessica opened her eyes, she saw that she had stepped inside a large cave and to her amazement she was completely dry.

The cave was dark except for the slight shimmer of sunlight coming through the waterfall. James was busy trying to light a fire in the middle of the cave. He motioned for them to sit on the small flat stones that formed a circle around the fire. Everyone was silent, even the cats whom Jessica had released from the bag. There was a solemn feeling in the air.

Once the fire was burning well and emitting welcome heat, James said in a low voice, "We must perform the ceremony now."

From inside the pocket of the long coat he was wearing, James pulled out a small, green velvet drawstring bag. From the bag he took what looked like different types of herbs and as he threw each of the herbs into the fire he quietly chanted. Jessica could barely hear what he was saying but she could tell that he was speaking a strange language. James then removed his coat and unbuttoned his coarse shirt, which he also removed. He stood up and leant over the fire. As he did so, he cupped his hands in front of him and brought them to his face as though he were washing himself in the smoke. Jessica was transfixed.

Then James said, "Jessica. Do you have the key?"

Jessica's mind went blank for a moment. Then she recalled the tiny silver key from her grandmother's letter. Jessica knew instinctively that this was the key James was asking for. Jessica removed her grandmother's locket from her neck and very carefully opened it. Inside, wrapped in a small piece of silk, was the silver key.

Jessica looked at the key before handing it silently to James. James took the key with a small bow of his head then, to Jessica's surprise, he threw it into the fire. The flames of the fire grew and sparked, sending out small flashes of light. Then, almost quicker than Jessica's eyes could really see, James put his hand into the fire and retrieved the key, which was glowing red from the heat. The heat seemed to have no impact on him. He then held the glowing key carefully between his thumb and forefinger and brought it closer to his chest. As he did so, the glow from the key seemed to spread out towards James' chest and his whole torso became a beautiful orange-red colour. Jessica then noticed for the first time that James had a very distinctive birthmark in the middle of his chest in the area of his heart. As she looked closer still, Jessica fancied that the birthmark was in the shape of a lock.

To Jessica's astonishment, James then held the key to his birthmark and as he did so, the key disappeared through his skin and into his chest. In the same instant a bright white light came pouring from his body and as it did so, his whole chest seemed to open to reveal his beating heart inside. Jessica was fascinated. Then James scooped up some of the ash from the fire with his hands and walked over to where the cats were sitting.

As he stood looking down at them he said, "It is time," and sprinkled some of the ash over them. The cats bowed their heads low and as they did so they turned back into the familiar ornament shapes that Jessica knew so well. James then picked up both the cats and held one in each of his hands. As he did so the cats became smaller and smaller until Jessica could barely see them. James then brought his hands closer to his chest and Jessica just saw each of the cats leap from his hands into his heart.

In the time it took Jessica to blink, James' chest had re-sealed and the white light was gone. All that was left was a slight glow on the man's face.

"It is done," James said. "They will be safe. For now, at least."

With that he put his shirt and coat back on and walked to the opening of the cave.

"It is time to get some rest," he said. "We have a long day ahead of us."

James and Tom then walked back through the waterfall and were gone.

Jessica could not speak for some time. She was in awe of what she had seen. When she had gathered her thoughts, Jessica turned to Rebecca and said, "Who is James?"

Rebecca laughed.

"Ah, he is many things," she replied mysteriously. "But first and foremost, he is a friend. He also happens to be my little brother."

"What?" said Jessica in disbelief. "But he is much older than you."

"That is what he would have you believe. But things are not always as they seem," said Rebecca.

"I'm starting to understand that!" said Jessica with a chuckle. "So how old are you?" asked Jessica. "You don't look much older than me, but earlier you said that you had not seen James for almost twenty-two years."

"Do not let the appearance of my young body fool you," said Rebecca. "I am older than you can even imagine. But that is not important. Everything is just an illusion anyway. You are older than you believe Jessica. You have been alive many times and have existed as many different people before. Remember that. It will serve you well when things seem too much for you and you feel that you cannot go on."

"I don't really understand it," said Jessica, "but I will try to remember."

"Now, let's get some sleep," said Rebecca, "we have a long journey tomorrow."

Despite the excitement of the day, Jessica slept very well and was woken in the morning by the glorious smell of cooking food. Jessica opened her eyes and realised that she was alone in the cave. She sat up, yawned loudly and stretched. She really had slept well. Jessica decided to go and investigate where the lovely smell was coming from. As she walked back through the waterfall she could see Rebecca just outside leaning over one of the boulders. She appeared to be cooking.

"Good morning," Rebecca called, "sleep well?"

"Like a log," replied Jessica. "I had the most wonderful dream."

"You dreamt?" asked Rebecca sounding concerned.

"Yes, why do you ask?" said Jessica.

Rebecca looked at her for a few seconds before replying.

"Oh, no reason. I'm sure it's nothing. Don't worry, forget I mentioned it."

But Jessica was worried. Even though Rebecca had tried to sound cheerful, she had a strange look in her eyes that made Jessica nervous.

"Well breakfast is ready," said Rebecca changing the subject. "I hope you like eggs and mushrooms. James found them fresh this morning."

"Where's James?" enquired Jessica. She had only just noticed that he was not there.

"He's gone off somewhere with Tom. I'm sure he'll be back soon," said Rebecca. "Now eat up, we've got to get going."

Rebecca left Jessica eating her breakfast and disappeared back through the waterfall.

Jessica finished her food and leant back against a boulder with her eyes closed, enjoying the warmth of the sun on her face. But her peace was disturbed by a rustling sound coming from the trees in front of her.

"Hello," said a voice.

Jessica looked up and was startled to see a young boy walking towards her. She looked around in the hope that Rebecca would re-appear from the cave.

"Did you enjoy your breakfast?" asked the boy.

"Yes, thank you," said Jessica.

Her initial feeling of panic at seeing the boy had almost gone. There was something reassuringly familiar about him. Just then, Tom the dog came bounding towards them from out of the forest. Tom headed straight for the boy, wagging his tail as he went and sat down next to him looking up at the boy's face.

"Hey, look, he knows you," said Jessica. "That's James' dog. Do you know James?"

The boy chuckled and replied, "Yes, I know James."

"Actually," said Jessica, "you look a bit like him. Is he your Dad?"

Before the boy could reply, Rebecca reappeared from the cave.

"Hi James," she said, "did you find out anything?"

"Your name is James too?" asked Jessica.

The boy laughed. "I am James," he said.

"What?!" said Jessica. "But James is old and you look about my age."

The boy sat down on the floor next to Jessica.

"It is my special gift," he said. "I can become any age I like. It helps me to see into the future. I just pick an age I want to be and there you go, I am that age and I have knowledge of all the things that will happen in the future when I'm that age."

"That's incredible," said Jessica. "So, what do you know now?" she asked.

"That we have to get going," replied James. "We're about to have company."

- CHAPTER SEVEN -

THE BOAT JOURNEY

Jessica was reluctant to leave the waterfall. It was so peaceful and beautiful and something in the way James had said, *we're about to have company*, scared her. James led the way with Jessica, Tom and Rebecca following. Jessica kept her hand on Tom's head the whole time. She felt calmer when she was next to him and got the feeling that he was a very good guard dog and would protect them.

The small group seemed to walk for a long time through the forest, but at last they left the wood and found themselves at the edge of what seemed to be a large lake.

"Now we must wait," announced James.

"For what?" asked Jessica.

"I saw that we should come to this place and that we would be met by someone. She will take us to the other side," James said.

"Are you ever wrong about what you see?" asked Jessica. "I'm not being funny, but surely things are changing all the time, so how do you know that what you have seen in the future will still be same when you actually get there?"

"I don't," replied James, "but that is the beauty of it. Nothing is set in stone, everything can be changed."

That was all he had to say on the matter.

And so they waited. And waited.

Jessica was beginning to think that they had come to the wrong place. She was starting to get very restless and absent-mindedly said, "Do you know who Mr Wicker is?"

"Mr Wicker!" repeated Rebecca in alarm.

"Shush!" ordered James. "Do not say that name in the open!"

Silence fell on the group; Tom whined pitifully. James motioned for Rebecca and Jessica to huddle closer to him.

"How do you know of this – person?" he asked.

"I've met him," whispered Jessica.

"What?! Have you seen him here?" asked Rebecca sounding shocked.

"No, no," said Jessica, "it was before, not here. It was in my world."

James and Rebecca exchanged glances.

"Go on," said James, encouraging Jessica to continue.

"The first time I saw him was about a year ago, just after Lily died. Then he was at my school," said Jessica, "he was chasing me just before I met you Rebecca."

"This is terrible news," said Rebecca. "I had no idea he could leave the dark realm. The Shadow Beings are stronger than we thought. And that means he has probably seen *me*!"

"You must tell us everything you remember," said James, "leave nothing out."

Jessica told James and Rebecca all about her encounters with Mr Wicker and the pair allowed her to talk without interruption. When she had finished, James and Rebecca left her and walked a few paces away so that she could not hear what they were saying. Their conversation was cut short by the arrival of a small boat.

Jessica could see that the captain of the boat was a very wrinkly old lady. She was dressed in dark, heavy clothing and her long white hair looked matted and dirty. She threw what looked like an anchor and rope over the side of the boat and into the water. Jessica noticed that the rope was not attached to the boat.

"Now then, now then," the old lady said, "who sent for me? Was it you?"

She pointed a bony finger in Jessica's direction.

"No madam, it was not," said Jessica.

"Humph, I see," the old lady said, "well, I shall be on my way then."

"Hang on," called Jessica, "I think my friend sent for you, here he comes now."

"Well make up your mind," said the old lady. "I haven't got all day you know."

James and Rebecca approached the boat.

"Hello," said James, "are you able to take us across?"

"It depends who wants to know," said the old lady and cackled loudly at her own reply.

Jessica noticed that she only had one rotten tooth left in her mouth. No one said anything so she continued, "What will you give me for safe passage?"

The group was silent, then Rebecca replied, "Here, you can have this."

She cupped her hands together and walked nearer to the woman.

"What is it?" asked the old lady, eyeing Rebecca suspiciously.

"It's called air," said Rebecca and opened her hands for the old lady to see.

There was nothing there.

"Ooooo," said the old lady with a twinkle in her eye. "I ain't never been given no air before. Get in, get in."

She motioned for them to get in the boat. Then the old lady spotted Tom.

"Argghh," she shrieked, "no wolves, no wolves in my boat, can't have no wolves," and proceeded to poke a long stick at Tom which she had produced from under her cloak.

"He is not a wolf," said Rebecca indignantly, "and if you don't let him get in the boat, I shall have to take the air back."

"Oh, no, no – please" whimpered the old lady.

Jessica felt sorry for her.

"Nice wolf can come on boat, nice wolf," crooned the old lady.

Once they were all safely on board, the boat started to move.

Jessica could not make out how the boat was moving as it had no motor, oars or sails. But she was starting to get used to the strangeness of this new place she had found herself in.

Jessica tried to make conversation with the old lady once or twice, but she seemed preoccupied with keeping an eye on Tom, so Jessica gave up. The boat journey passed without incident and Jessica was beginning to feel quite relaxed once more. She could see the shore they were aiming for in the distance and estimated that they would be in the boat for another twenty minutes or so. Then the boat came to an abrupt stop.

"Here you are," said the old lady, "all off, all off."

She began poking Rebecca with her stick.

"Hey!" shouted Rebecca. "Watch where you put that stick! What do you mean all off? We haven't arrived anywhere yet, we're in the middle of the lake!"

"That's it, all off," repeated the old lady. "That's as far as I go. The others will take you the rest of the way."

With that, the old lady lent over the side of the boat and stuck her head in the water. Rebecca, Jessica and James all looked at each other.

The old lady's head was underwater for so long that Jessica began to worry that she might drown. She tapped her on the back. The old lady stood up straight with such force that her soaking wet hair flicked back and drenched her passengers.

"Ooh, hee hee, so sorry," the old lady chuckled, "but don't worry, they're on their way."

The group did not have time to ask who was on their way, as two large heads surfaced from the water and looked into the boat.

"Ah, here they are," said the old lady. "They will take you the rest of the way."

Jessica had been studying the heads and realised that they belonged to two giant green turtles.

"Before we go," said James to the old lady, "may I ask if you know how to get to the Full Moon Inn from here?"

The old lady thought for a moment then replied, "You need to get on the road towards Watchamacallit, but before you get there you

need to take
a left at the
crossroads and go to
Whatsit. When you get there, you
need to go to the Doobery and ask them the way
to Somewhereoranother – that's where the inn
is. But they'll be able to tell you at the Doobery.
Goodbye and thanks for the air."

James was too polite to say anything to the
old lady. Instead he turned his attention to
climbing on the back of one of the huge turtles
who was waiting patiently next to the boat.
Tom followed him and Rebecca and Jessica
climbed onto the back of the second turtle.
They all waved goodbye to the old lady and

shouted, "Thank you!" but she did not seem to hear them.

"Did you understand any of her directions?" Jessica asked James.

"No," he laughed, "but I'm sure we'll find someone who can help us!"

The turtles swam very slowly and gently towards the shore so as not to get their passengers too wet. Jessica thought it was a marvellous way to travel. The shells of the beautiful turtles were so large that she and Rebecca had plenty of room to lie at full stretch on their backs. Tom was obviously enjoying the ride too and barked with excitement every now and then.

Once the turtles reached the shore they climbed up the bank to allow their passengers to step down. They all thanked the turtles for the ride and watched as the beautiful creatures slipped back into the water and disappeared below the surface.

The four friends stood on the bank of the lake for some time, each waiting for the other to make a decision as to which direction they should take.

"Well, this won't do," said James scratching his head, "let's just walk straight and see where it takes us."

"Hang on," said Jessica, "where do you think that goes?"

She pointed at a small path through some trees that they had not noticed before.

"Well, that's as good a way as any," said James.

They were just about to step on the path and continue their journey when a voice announced, "This is the road to Watchamacallit."

They looked round, trying to locate the owner of the voice.

"I'm down here," said the voice sounding rather disgruntled.

As they continued looking round, Jessica noticed a small worm by the side of the path. She bent down to take a closer look.

"I'm sorry," she said, "but did you say something?"

"Yes, it was I," replied the worm. "You are about to set foot on the road to Watchamacallit."

"Oh, I see," said Jessica laughing, "we thought it was nonsense, you know, a nothing name like, I don't know, Thingymajig."

"I happen to come from Thingymajig," replied the worm indignantly.

"I'm sorry," Jessica said apologetically, "and thank you for the information. This is the road we need. Can you tell me, is there a real place called Whatsit?"

The worm looked at Jessica with contempt and as he turned his back on her and began to wriggle away, he shot her a look and said, "My dentist lives there."

"Oh dear," said Jessica to the others, "I think I offended him."

"Don't worry," said Rebecca, "the worms are known for being very sensitive. No sense of humour!"

With that the four friends set off once more along the road towards Watchamacallit.

Just as the old lady had said, they reached a crossroads with a signpost and Whatsit was clearly marked with an arrow pointing left. They continued along the path for some time until it came to an abrupt end.

"I guess we have to go up there," James said.

He pointed towards the top of a steep hill in the distance. Once they reached the bottom of the hill they began to walk up. There were tiny steps cut into the earth in a zigzag pattern which made it easier to climb. The hillside was covered with lush green grass and small clumps of brightly coloured flowers dotted here and there. Tom ran ahead of the others and when he got to the top of the hill he began to bark ferociously.

Rebecca, James and Jessica ran the rest of the way up to find out what it was Tom was barking at. They joined Tom on top of the hill and as they looked down onto the other side, they were dismayed by what they saw. The whole hillside and surrounding valley was black and smoking as though it had been set on fire. There was a horrible singed smell lingering in the air. Not one blade of grass or flower had survived. They could also see in the distance the charred remains of what had probably once been a small village.

"Oh no," groaned Rebecca, "how has this happened? Who would do such a thing?"

"I'll give you three guesses," said James. "This is the start of it then. The devastation has begun. We must press on, it's not safe here."

They picked their way carefully down the blackened hillside and headed in the direction of the village they had seen from the top. They finally came upon a half-burnt sign lying on the ground and could just make out the letters *SIT*.

"I suppose this is Whatsit then," said Rebecca dejectedly.

"Or was," added James. "Come on, let's see if anyone's here."

- CHAPTER EIGHT -

PORSKIN

The village was deserted. From what was left of the homes, Jessica could see that it had probably been a lovely place. Now it was in ruins.

"We must be careful," said James quietly, "we may not be alone."

They cautiously walked through the village until they came upon a large building that looked as though it had once been very grand. Above the doorway was a sign, which read, *The Doobery*.

"Let's go in," said Rebecca.

"I think you and Jessica should stay out here," said James. "I'll see what I can find out. Tom, look after them."

Rebecca and Jessica reluctantly agreed. James approached the building slowly, pushing open what was left of the door and went inside.

"It's really creepy," said Jessica.

"I know," replied Rebecca. "I don't have a good feeling about this."

Just then they noticed that Tom was standing very still and his ears were pointing up as though he were listening to something. Then he began to whine.

"What is it boy?" asked Rebecca.

"I think he can hear something," said Jessica.

"Come on, I'm not staying out here," said Rebecca, "let's go and find James."

The two girls and Tom got inside the building just in time, for a group of fifteen to twenty agents of the Shadow Beings suddenly appeared. They were a filthy, loathsome group. A band of the most frightening, wicked, nightmarish characters you can imagine. The leader appeared to have the body of a man with the head of a wolf. His lank, greasy black hair covered most of his face, including the cavity where his left eye had once been, but it could not hide the long, gnarled snout, which was full of sharp teeth. Spit and froth oozed from his mouth when he spoke. He sniffed the air.

"They have been here," he snarled. "But there is a new one, one I've not smelt before. The Master will be pleased. Leave the new one to me. You may kill the others."

The hideous group whooped and shouted with delight and blood lust and entered the building behind Rebecca and Jessica.

"James, where are you?" Rebecca called in a loud whisper.

Tom barked and looked at the girls to indicate that they should follow him. The building was in tatters. Jessica assumed from what was left that it had once been some sort of meeting place or theatre as she could see the remains of lots of chairs and a raised area at one end of a large hall. They could see James through a doorway standing in a room at the other end of the hall. Tom barked again and ran towards him. The girls followed. James looked up when he heard Tom bark.

"I thought I said to wait outside," said James.

"I know," replied Rebecca, "but Tom could sense something and we didn't want to stay out there."

"Have you found anything?" asked Jessica.

"Only this," said James.

He handed Jessica a piece of paper. It was covered in a scrawl, which Jessica found difficult to read.

They have come upon us. Without warning. They have come. Looking for the Gatekeepers. We are ruined. Those who were able to have fled. Others have perished. The time has come. The time has come. All is lost. Where are the Gatekeepers? Guardian. Guardian. Guar –

The writing trailed off. They were silent, then Tom began to snarl.

"We must leave," said James.

"I think not," said a voice.

They had been so engrossed in the letter, that they had not noticed they were no longer alone. Jessica thought she was going to faint. Never before had she seen such vile creatures.

"What are we going to do?!" she said with a cry.

"Rebecca, you must do something!" shouted James. "Use your gift!"

Rebecca was terrified.

"I, I, can't," she stammered.

"You must! You must try," urged James pleading with her.

"Jessica. We must make her laugh." James said.

"What?" exclaimed Jessica. "What are you talking about?"

The group of bloodthirsty creatures moved closer to them. Tom was now standing in between them and his friends, teeth bared, snarling and barking.

"We must make her laugh," said James again with more urgency. "Tell a joke or something, anything to make her laugh."

Jessica was confused, she had no idea what James was talking about.

"Quickly!" cried James.

Jessica racked her brain, she couldn't think! Then it popped into her head. It was a joke Lily had once told her. But it seemed ridiculous. Now was not the time to be telling jokes!

"Jess!" James implored.

"Ok, ok. Here goes," Jessica shouted. She took a deep breath and said, "Why did the chewing gum cross the road? Because it was stuck to the chicken!"

There was silence for a moment. Jessica's heart was in her mouth. Then it started slowly. First there was a smile, then a snigger, followed by a loud giggle. Then it erupted. Jessica put her hands over her ears. Rebecca was laughing and laughing. But it was no ordinary laugh; it was the loudest laugh Jessica had ever heard.

Before she knew what was happening, more laughter erupted. It was all around them and when Jessica looked, their revolting would-be captors were beside themselves with laughter. But they looked as though they were in agony. Their faces were grimaced in pain. Some were holding their heads in their hands and others had their arms wrapped around their bellies. They were incapable of moving as they were laughing so much.

"Come on!" shouted James. "We have to leave, they won't stay like this for long."

As the four raced to the door, Jessica noticed with horror that some of the creatures were laughing so much that their heads had ripped off and their sides were splitting. It was a gory scene.

Once outside, they ran and ran and ran.

"I need to stop," said Jessica breathlessly. "I can't run anymore."

"We must keep going," said James.

"I can't, I really can't," said Jessica.

"Pssst, come with me, quick," said a voice.

They looked round, alarmed that they had not seen the stranger approach them.

"Stay back," warned James.

"You must trust me," said the voice, "I can help you."

"Why should we trust you?" said Rebecca.

"Do you have a choice?" asked the stranger.

They eyed him suspiciously then Tom slowly approached the stranger, his tail wagging slightly. The man wore a long cloak and his face was hidden from view by a length of material which was wrapped around his head. They could just make out two sparkling brown eyes and part of the stranger's mouth through gaps in the material.

"Please," he implored, "please come with me."

They reluctantly followed the stranger who led them away from the road and into an area surrounded by enormous rocks and boulders.

"I will take you underground," the stranger said. "They may not be able to follow us that way."

Jessica felt uneasy. She was not sure what she thought of this person yet. He was odd, the way the top of his body was all hunched over and she didn't like the fact that she couldn't see his face.

"You want to get to Somewhereoranother, is that right?" he enquired.

"Yes, how did you know that?" asked James.

The man chuckled, "I know of many things."

"That doesn't really answer my question," said James defensively.

"Looking for the Gatekeeper are you?" the man said.

"Yes!" shouted Jessica. "Do you know about the Gatekeeper?"

"Jess!" said James and gave her a look that said, "be quiet!"

Jessica stayed silent.

"Last seen at the Full Moon Inn it was," said the stranger.

"That's where we want to go," said James.

"Porskin can take you there," replied the man.

"Is Porskin your name?" asked Rebecca.

"Yes, yes, old Porskin can take you."

After that the man fell silent.

The group followed Porskin through a series of underground tunnels and caves which were lit by strange little lights that seemed to be everywhere.

"What are these lights?" Jessica asked, breaking the silence.

"They're the glow worms," replied Porskin. "They are our friends. Only light up when there's good about. Go out when there's bad. Only small, but they try to help."

Jessica was fascinated by the lights and felt better after what Porskin had said. If he was not to be trusted she thought, then surely the lights would go out?

The group stayed close to Porskin. No one wanted to get lost in the maze of tunnels. Jessica thought it remarkable that he knew his way around them so well. It was slow going, as Porskin could not walk very fast. As well as his hunched back, he seemed to have difficulty with his legs and walking seemed to be painful for him. They were patient though and grateful for the help.

At last they could see an opening in front of them and were glad to see the sunlight pouring through. When the group emerged from the tunnels they were amazed to find that they had climbed out of what looked like an old wooden barrel! Jessica could not believe it. She looked around the barrel and was even able to push it slightly. It did not appear to be fixed to the ground and she could find no trace of a hole or anything. *Strange*, she thought to herself. *But I don't know why I'm still surprised by these things after all I've seen!*

Once they had gathered themselves together, the group looked around and found that they were standing in the middle of a very busy little town.

"Well, here we are," said Porskin, "this is Somewhereoranother."

There was a lot of hustle and bustle in the town and Jessica thought what a contrast it was to Whatsit. She felt sad to think that Whatsit had been like this once and now it was destroyed.

"Right, we need to get to the Full Moon Inn," said James.

"I'll take you to it, then I must leave you," said Porskin.

They walked some way through the town and Jessica was fascinated by all the different characters she saw.

"Well, here it is," said Porskin, "and goodbye."

He went to leave.

"Hang on," said James, "I was expecting something a little, erm, bigger than this!"

The group were standing outside what looked like an old fashioned, outside toilet shed. There was a sign hanging on the door which read, *Full Moon Inn.*

"Ah, don't let the size fool you," said Porskin with a chuckle. "Off I go and goodbye I'm gone," he added and shuffled away.

James looked puzzled.

"Well, there's only one thing for it," said Rebecca. "We had better go in."

Rebecca pushed open the door of the inn and stepped inside, followed closely by the others.

They all gasped. Once inside, the inn was cavernous! Jessica laughed. She had never been inside such a large place! Just to check, she stepped back outside and, sure enough, the outside of the inn was only the size of a very small toilet shed.

"No dogs allowed in here," someone shouted.

"Sorry Tom," said James, "can you wait outside? There's a good boy. I'll bring you some water and something to eat."

Tom went outside as he had been asked, but was not happy about being separated from the others.

Whilst Rebecca and James found somewhere to sit and ordered something to eat and drink, Jessica was taking in her new surroundings. The inn was a vibrant, lively place and there was a lot going on to keep her occupied. Almost every table in the Full Moon was taken and everyone was making the most of the hospitality. The inn was buzzing with conversation and laughter. Jessica felt very comfortable there and suddenly became aware that she felt very, very tired. The day's events were beginning to catch up with her.

"You sit down and rest," said James to Rebecca and Jessica. "I'm going to find out if they have somewhere we can stay tonight. I think we should get some rest before we move on. I also want to find out if the Gatekeeper is still here."

The girls watched as James went to speak to the proprietor of the inn. Jessica decided it was a good time to question Rebecca about what had happened earlier in Whatsit.

"B?" she asked. "How did we manage to get away from those awful creatures?" She shuddered at the memory of them. "I know they were laughing," she continued, "but how did it happen?"

"That's my special gift," Rebecca said. "Like James is able to become any age and see into the future, somehow, when I laugh it seems to render wickedness helpless, for a while at least."

"Do you have any other gifts?" asked Jessica.

"I'm not sure," replied Rebecca. "These things seem to just happen when you really need them. I can't switch it on though, it just happens, but it has helped me out of quite a few sticky situations. It's almost like it is not coming from me, rather it comes through me, as though someone else were doing it. It's difficult to explain. I suppose if I really needed help another time, maybe I would get a different gift."

"Do you think I have any gifts?" asked Jessica.

"I believe you have many special gifts. You'll see," said Rebecca with a warm smile.

James returned to where the girls were sitting with their food and drinks and the trio eagerly tucked in. They had not realised how hungry they were.

"Well," said James, "some good news. We have a room for tonight, but no information. The landlord said he didn't know anything about the Gatekeeper and denied that the cat had even been at the inn. Can you believe that! I'm not sure he was telling the truth, in fact, he looked a bit scared when I asked him."

"Maybe he has heard about what happened in Whatsit," said Rebecca.

"Maybe," replied James deep in thought. "He did say that someone was coming to the inn later though who may be able to help us. I think for now I will leave you and see what I can find out."

"Be careful," said Rebecca, "I still feel shaken up after earlier and I don't think it will be long before the agents track us here."

With that, James bade them farewell and left the inn.

"Do you mind if I go up to our room?" asked Jessica. "I'm feeling so tired, if I just have a little sleep I might feel better."

"Of course," said Rebecca, "you go up and I'll join you shortly. I'm going to speak to a few people here to see if they know anything."

Jessica was only too grateful when she finally sunk onto the bed in the room of the inn. It was not long before she had fallen into a deep, deep sleep.

- CHAPTER NINE -

THE DREAVERS

"Where's Jessica?"

Rebecca was startled by James' sudden appearance. He looked extremely anxious and was out of breath as though he had been running.

"She went up to the room to get some sleep," replied Rebecca. "Is everything alright, you look terrible?"

James' face turned a shade greyer.

"We must get to her. I've had an awful vision," he said. "I went to the future to try to get some information on what we should do next and I saw, I saw…"

"What? What did you see?" implored Rebecca.

"It was the Dreavers. They were here and they had taken her," said James quietly.

"Oh no," said Rebecca with horror, "we must get to her before they come!"

James and Rebecca ran through the inn and up the stairs to the room where Jessica was sleeping. They opened the door and frantically searched the room. The only evidence that Jessica had been there was an unmade bed.

"We're too late!" shouted Rebecca. "They've got her, we're too late!" She began to cry.

"Wait, wait," said James, trying to sound calm. "Let's not jump to conclusions, I may have got it wrong."

"No," cried Rebecca, "look! "

She bent down and picked up an object she had seen sticking out from under the bed. It was Jessica's locket.

"She would never go anywhere without this. Poor Jessica. It's all my fault, I should have stayed with her. I thought she would be safe here. And we were supposed to be protecting her."

Rebecca fell sobbing into James' arms.

"We must be strong," said James, trying to sound more positive than he felt. "We must find out where they have taken her. They can't have gone far. If we leave now we may be able to catch up with them. Tom should be able to track them."

Jessica had no idea what had happened to her. She was still fast asleep and unaware; and that is how she would remain forever, a prisoner of the Dreavers. The Dreavers or Dream Thieves were a fiendish creation of the Shadow Beings. They received sustenance by feeding off the dreams of the unsuspecting. The Dreavers sensed those who were dreaming and stole their vulnerable prey from their beds whilst they were asleep. Once safely in their grasp, the sleeper was destined to remain a captive of the dream world forever, whilst the Dreavers watched their dreams as you or I would watch a film.

The Dreavers were particularly pleased with their new acquisition. They had sensed that there was something different about Jessica and had been alerted to her presence by her strong dream signals. It would only be a matter of time before the Shadow Beings became aware that they were holding her. And then Jessica's story would be over…

In the meantime, James, Rebecca and Tom were trying their best to track Jessica and to find out where she had been taken. It seemed like an impossible task as the Dreavers were able to fly and this made it difficult for Tom to pick up their scent. They could not give up on their friend though. The whole future depended on them finding Jessica. They had to have hope that they would succeed.

Completely unaware of her predicament, Jessica was having a dreadful dream. It was all about being chased and taken prisoner by agents of the Shadow Beings and of the world being cast into darkness forever. The Dreavers were enjoying watching this dream immensely. They received great pleasure from seeing others suffer in the dream world. The worse the nightmare, the more they enjoyed it. But their enjoyment was short lived.

Jessica's dream changed suddenly and she found herself standing in a grassy meadow. She was completely surrounded by butterflies of every colour and size imaginable. Jessica dreamt that she was holding her hands out in front of her and the butterflies were landing on her and covering her whole body. There were so many butterflies that, for a time, Jessica could not be seen in their midst. The Dreavers were infuriated. This dream was far too pleasant for their liking and they lost interest in watching Jessica. They would wait until she dreamt of something a little less wholesome.

It was during this lapse in the Dreavers' attention that Lily appeared to Jessica. Hidden by the butterflies, she remained unseen by the Dreavers.

"Jessica, you must listen carefully, I don't have much time," said Lily, whispering into Jessica's ear.

"Lily, where am I? It is so beautiful," Jessica said.

"You are dreaming," replied Lily, "but you have been captured. Now you must do as I say. You must clear your mind completely. You must try not to think about anything. It is important that you do not dream otherwise they will not wake you. If you have to think of something, imagine white light, nothing but white light. I will try to contact James and Rebecca to tell them where you are."

"Lily, Lily!" Jessica called.

But her grandmother had gone. The butterflies also disappeared and Jessica found herself in a black, damp pit. There were strange, terrifying noises all around her. The Dreavers tuned in once more.

"It's just a dream, it's just a dream," she said to herself. "I must not think of anything."

With that, Jessica was no longer in the pit. Instead she was bathed in white light, all around her, nothing but white light. The Dreavers were furious and realised that someone must have warned her.

They waited and waited to see if Jessica's will would break, but it did not. She just kept thinking of white light. The Dreavers' patience ran out and they decided to wake her in the hope that they could force her to dream again. If they did not succeed, they would kill her. She was no good to them like this. They removed Jessica from the contraption she had been connected to, which kept her asleep and allowed them to watch her dreams. For a moment Jessica thought she was still dreaming, but when she realised that she was in fact awake, she screamed at the top of her voice.

The Dreavers were the most frightening things she had ever seen. She was surrounded by eight of them. They were tall, thin creatures with bald heads that seemed too big for their bodies. Their pale, translucent skin was so thin that Jessica could make out their bony skeletons underneath. They had huge eyes, large toothless, gummy mouths and a hole in the middle of their faces where their noses should have been. They wore no clothes from what Jessica could make out and had black leathery bat-like

wings on their
backs. They were
prodding her with their
long, bony fingers to wake
her up.

"We knows what you's trying to do," one
of them said to Jessica. "We knows you's trying
not to dream. You's no good to us with no
dreams. If yous don't dream we kills you. Or
worse still, we takes you to Brain Drainer. He'd
love to have yous as one of his zombies."

The group let out a series of ghastly cheers and cries.

"So yous be good," the creature continued, "and stops dreaming in whites and we lets yous live."

"O-o-ok," stammered Jessica; she was terrified of the unearthly ghouls.

The Dreavers were just about to re-attach Jessica to the machine when she heard a blood-curdling scream coming from somewhere behind her. Chaos ensued. One of the creatures was shouting, "It's him, it's him!"

Others were just screaming and trying to run. In the confusion, Jessica was dragged to the floor. The last thing she remembered seeing before she fainted, was a grotesquely deformed face close to hers. But the kind eyes. Kind eyes.

"Come now little one, drink this. You've had quite a shock."

Jessica recognised the gentle voice and gratefully took a sip of the warm, sweet liquid being offered to her. Jessica drifted in and out of consciousness before finally coming around. She was lying on the floor on comfortable cushions and was covered in layers of blankets.

She appeared to be in some sort of hut. It was warm and cosy and she felt very safe. She could just make out a dark shape in the corner. As the figure turned to face her she realised that it was Porskin.

"Hello there sleepy head," he said.

"Oh Porskin," Jessica cried, "I'm so glad to see you! Did you get me away from those awful creatures?"

Porskin chuckled.

"Yes, yes," he said, "gave them quite a fright I did."

"You gave *them* a fright," said Jessica, "they almost scared me to death! What are they?"

"They're Dreavers," said Porskin. "Nasty things they are, but no match for old Porskin. I don't think they'll be troubling us again for a while."

Porskin pulled up a chair and sat beside Jessica.

"Here, eat this," he said handing Jessica a bowl of what looked like tree bark.

"What is it?" she asked, turning her nose up slightly.

"Good stuff. Try it. Help get strength back," said Porskin.

Jessica reluctantly tried the food and was amazed at how good it tasted.

When she had finished eating she turned

to Porskin and said, "Was that you I saw just before I fainted?"

There was a moment's silence then Porskin replied quietly, "Yes, it was Porskin you saw."

"What happened to your face?" asked Jessica.

"Was born like it," replied Porskin sadly.

"May I, may I see your face?" Jessica asked.

Jessica thought she saw Porskin frown as he hesitated for a moment. Then slowly he began to unwind the material that covered his face and head. Jessica held her breath. Once the covering was removed, Jessica could see the full extent of his deformity.

His whole head and face were covered in what looked like red, fleshy scars, as though his skin had been burnt in a terrible fire. A few strands of hair stuck out from his head and his nose was badly contorted and bent over to the right side of his face. Jessica looked at him fully in the face for a long time. She then held out one of her hands to touch him. He flinched as her hand came nearer.

"Don't be afraid," she said.

Her hand made contact with Porskin's face and she tenderly stroked his cheek.

"I think you are beautiful," she said to him. "Thank you for saving me."

"Get some more rest now," said Porskin, "tomorrow you must find the others."

He turned away so that Jessica would not see the tears streaming down his face.

In the morning Jessica awoke feeling refreshed and energised. She stretched and yawned loudly before getting up to look for Porskin. He was nowhere to be seen. Jessica went outside.

"Porskin!" she called, but there was no reply.

Jessica went back inside the hut and found a small bundle of food on the table with a note.

For your journey.
Life carries on
And death has no hold
There is a secret
Where the water is cold.

She decided that Porskin had gone for the moment and that it was up to her to continue her journey alone. Jessica had no idea which way she should go, so thought it best to just follow a small pathway she could see just through the trees. It was a beautiful day and Jessica felt as though her nightmare of the day before was a million miles away.

She thought for a few seconds, then said out loud, "The sea. I need to go to the sea."

- CHAPTER TEN -
MERFOLK

Jessica felt as though she had been walking along the path for at least two hours and still had no idea if she was heading in the right direction. She decided to have a break and eat some of the food that Porskin had left for her. But just as she had settled herself on a log and was about to start eating, she thought she heard a buzzing sound. She listened intently for a few minutes in silence and was about to tuck into her sandwich once more when she heard the buzzing again.

"Hello," Jessica called out nervously, "who's there?"

She heard the buzzing again.

It seemed to be coming from somewhere on her left so she decided to leave the path to investigate. Jessica looked all around her but could not see what was making the noise. She was just about to head back to the path when something flew past her head and tickled her ear.

"Hey!" Jessica shouted. "Who did that?"

Out of the corner of her eye Jessica just caught a flash of something fast and blue. She waited and waited but nothing else happened. Just as she decided she was imagining things and had started to make her way back to the path, the most enormous dragonfly Jessica had ever seen emerged from behind a tree. It was the size of a very large eagle and its wings were beating so fast that they were a blur. It eyes were huge and round and its body seemed to be coloured with every shade of blue imaginable. It was beautiful. Jessica was in awe.

As she stood staring at the dragonfly, it began to fly wildly above Jessica's head, twisting and turning, flying upside down, making all sorts of loops and patterns. Jessica thought it was going to crash into her so she put her arms protectively over her head and crouched down low to the floor. When it seemed that the dragonfly had come to a stop on a nearby tree branch, Jessica

slowly
stood up and
was amazed by what she saw.

In the space above her head where the dragonfly had been moments before, were some words in dazzling iridescent blue, just floating in the air.

My name is Ashley. I am a friend. Follow me.

Before Jessica had time to question how the dragonfly had written the words, it took off from the tree branch it had been resting on and started to fly swiftly away.

"Wait! Ashley, wait for me," Jessica called

as she ran to keep up with the dragonfly. She barely had time to collect her food from the log where she had left it, before the dragonfly was almost out of sight ahead of her on the path.

Jessica had to jog most of the way to ensure that she kept up with Ashley. He would land on a branch from time to time and turn his head in her direction to make sure that she was still behind him.

Just when she thought she couldn't go any further, Jessica thought she could hear the sound of waves crashing on a beach. Up ahead, through a gap in the trees, Jessica caught a glimpse of something golden, and before she knew it, she was running on beautiful, soft sand.

"The sea, thank goodness!" Jessica exclaimed and sank down onto the sand, exhausted.

Ashley flew to where Jessica was sitting, landed gently on her arm and looked at her with his large dragonfly eyes.

"I've never seen a dragonfly quite as large as you before," Jessica said to Ashley, "or as beautiful," she added. "Thank you for showing me the way. I'm not quite sure what I'm meant to do now though."

Just then, Jessica heard someone laughing. Then the sound of several people laughing. She looked up and thought she saw someone swimming in the sea, but the reflection of the sun on the water's surface was so bright she could not see clearly. Then from out of the water came a huge lumbering turtle. It was the turtle she had ridden on before! The turtle looked at her and instinctively she knew that she had to go with him. Balancing Ashley gently on her arm, she carefully climbed onto the turtle's back and the marine giant waded back into the sea.

Jessica felt perfectly safe, even when the turtle dived under the water. Initially she held her breath until she noticed that lots of bubbles were coming out of Ashley's mouth. Then she realised to her astonishment that they could breathe underwater! The turtle took them down, down, down towards the bottom of the sea. Jessica looked round, taking in the beauty of all the sea life that surrounded them.

It was then that she saw the mermaids. There were a dozen or so fair maidens of the sea, each one more beautiful than any person Jessica had ever seen. They waved to Jessica and Ashley and started to sing. They had the loveliest voices and Jessica felt as though a great weight were being lifted from her. The mermaids followed the turtle until he eventually arrived at their destination. Jessica had been so busy looking at the mermaids that she had not noticed the vast underwater city below them. The turtle swam up to an enormous door, which opened as they approached. Once inside, the turtle came to a stop to allow his passengers to climb off his back.

Jessica and Ashley found themselves standing in the middle of what looked like a ballroom. It was a sumptuous room and was decorated on all sides with brightly coloured stained-glass windows. The ceiling was so high it reminded Jessica of a grand cathedral she had once visited. At the far end of the room, a set of double doors opened and hundreds of merfolk poured inside. Jessica was in awe. They were incredible beings.

A hush fell upon the room and from the midst of the throng of merfolk, two in particular came forward to greet Jessica and Ashley. One was a merman, the other a mermaid and each was wearing a crown on their head. Jessica guessed that they were the king and queen of the merfolk.

"Welcome to our kingdom," said the king, his voice had a rich tone. "We have been expecting you for some time now."

He bowed low before Jessica. The queen took a step nearer to Jessica and held something out towards her. It was a giant water lily. She too bowed and said, "We have been safeguarding this, waiting for you to return. Now it must be given back to you."

Jessica solemnly took the water lily from the queen. To her delight, Jessica saw that sitting on top of the water lily, wrapped in seaweed was an ornament in the shape of a cat!

The cat was made from different pieces of coloured shell and had two perfect, green emerald eyes. Jessica clutched the cat close to her.

"Life carries on and death has no hold," said the queen. "Now, let us celebrate the return of the Guardian!"

She clapped her hands and instantly music began to play in the ballroom. Then all the merfolk burst into song and filled the middle of the room where they began to dance. It was a joyous scene.

Jessica and Ashley danced and danced and lost all track of time. Jessica could have happily stayed there forever, but she knew that she

had to return to the surface and continue her journey. She thanked the king and queen for keeping the cat safe and for returning it to her. She and Ashley then climbed back onto the shell of the turtle and waved goodbye to the beautiful merfolk, as they swam back through the door and out into the open sea.

Jessica's spirits were much lifted and as the turtle reached the shore she actually felt quite positive once again. She was even happier when she realised, as her head popped above the surface of the water, that waiting for them on the beach were Rebecca, James and Tom!

"And where have you been?" asked Rebecca with a laugh.

"Becky!" shouted Jessica and ran to her friend. "James!" Jessica was thrilled to be reunited with them and the three hugged each other tightly. "I've got so much to tell you," said Jessica.

"So have we," said James.

"I've got one of the cats," said Jessica with delight, "the merfolk had it."

"That's brilliant," said Rebecca. "Who's this?" she asked pointing to Ashley.

"This is Ashley," replied Jessica. "He found me in the forest and showed me the way to the sea. I would never have found it without him. I'm so happy to see you, I didn't think I would find you again," Jessica cried as she hugged Rebecca once more.

"Come on," said James, "I know somewhere not far from here where we can go to talk."

They followed James across the beach until they came to a small, dry cave. It was then that Jessica noticed for the first time, that James looked older than when she had seen him last.

Once inside the cave, James decided it was best to perform the fire ceremony before they did anything else. So, just as before, a fire was lit and James opened his heart to allow the third cat to enter. After that, the friends talked and talked as Jessica told them all about what had happened to her since they were last together. Rebecca and James were amazed by all that Jessica had been through.

"You poor thing," said Rebecca, "those Dreavers sound dreadful. You are so brave. And it was lucky Porskin was there, I wonder where he is now? Before I forget Jess, here, this is for you."

Rebecca handed Jessica her locket that she had dropped in the room of the Full Moon Inn.

"I hadn't even realised I didn't have it," said Jessica. "Thank you for looking after it for me."

She put the locket back round her neck.

"So how did you know where to find me?" asked Jessica.

"Well," said Rebecca, "first of all Lily came to me in a dream. She said that you were in trouble and that we had to find you. She showed me where you were, but when James and I got there you had already gone. Luckily there was no sign of the Dreavers when we arrived. Then," she continued, "James became a bit older and went to the future to try and find out where you were."

"Yes," said James continuing the story, "I saw that you were with the merfolk and that's what brought us here. But there's more," he said seriously. "I saw cats Jess, hundreds of cats. They were being rounded up from all over the land by agents of the Shadow Beings. They were being held and were about to be killed! The Shadow Beings believe that if they destroy all the cats they can find, then maybe they'll end up killing one or more of the Gatekeepers in the process. The future of all our worlds is hanging in the balance. It could go either way. The Shadow Beings grow stronger by the day and unless we find the other two Gatekeepers, I'm, I don't know—"

"We'll find them!" announced Jessica with more determination than she actually felt. But it seemed to do the trick. Rebecca and James were buoyed by her sudden optimism.

"Yes, that's the spirit," said Rebecca, "come on, let's get going!"

- CHAPTER ELEVEN -

THE TIGGLER

The three brave friends left the beautiful beach with Tom and Ashley and set off in a northerly direction. They were happy to be together once more, but deep down each of them felt apprehensive about what was ahead of them. However, no one wanted to spoil the optimistic mood that was now upon them and their concerns remained unspoken.

Before long the landscape began to change dramatically. All around them there was evidence of the work the Shadow Beings' agents. They were no longer walking through luscious greenery, meadows and woodland. Just as in Whatsit, there were signs of destruction and mayhem all around. Once beautiful areas had been reduced to burnt and stinking wasteland. Whole villages had been destroyed and were now deserted. There was an eerie stillness in the air. Even the birds seemed to have left. They did not encounter anyone along the way and Jessica guessed that the people had either fled or been captured. Worse still, they may have been killed. The mood of the group became sombre and they walked in silence.

They had been walking for some time when Tom began to bark and ran ahead of the others.

"What is it boy?" called James.

Tom had disappeared over the brow of a hill and the others ran to catch up with him. As they reached the top of the hill they could see that Tom was heading for a small village. It was intact and did not seem to have been touched by the fires.

"That's odd," said Jessica. "Why would they spare this one?"

"Mmm, I'm not sure," replied Rebecca, "it does seem strange. Let's have a look."

"Be careful," warned James, "I do not think it is safe here."

James, Rebecca, Jessica and Ashley cautiously made their way towards the village. Tom was busy sniffing around and was slowly edging nearer and nearer to one particular shelter. When he got to the door he began to whine and scratch at it with his paws. James approached the door and slowly, carefully pushed it open. Rebecca gasped. Inside were at least thirty small children. They had all been bound with rope and were sitting on the floor. As James walked inside they all began to cower and some started to cry.

"It's ok," James said in a kind voice to reassure them, "we'll help you, don't worry."

Rebecca and Jessica joined him inside the shelter and were horrified that someone could have done this.

"Who did this to you?" James asked an older looking child.

"I-it was, it was," the child stammered, "it was the dark ones. They took our parents but said they were leaving us as bait."

Then it suddenly dawned on James. They had been lured there!

"Quick!" he shouted to the girls. "We have to get out of here, it's a trap!"

But it was too late. They were already surrounded by agents of the Shadow Beings.

Before they knew what was happening, James, Rebecca and Jessica had been seized. Tom was beside himself and was biting and clawing any of the agents he could get to.

"Tom!" shouted James. "You must go for help. Run boy, run!"

Tom did not look back. He narrowly missed being caught and ran for his life. He had to get help for his friends!

"Rebecca!" called James. "Use your laugh, you must use your laugh!"

But Rebecca could not. She had already been bound and gagged by the agents and was helpless. Jessica was terrified. *It's all over, it's all over*, she thought.

Then she saw him. She wasn't sure at first, but as he drew closer she knew. It was Mr Wicker!

"We meet again young lady," he purred, his thin lips contorted into a leering smile. "You have been more of a challenge than, erherm, I first gave you credit for. But you have escaped from me for the last time. I believe you have something I want. If you give the Gatekeepers to me I will show pity on your, erherm, friendssss," he hissed in her face. "If not, they will suffer a long and painful death. The choice is yours."

"I, I don't know what you are talking about," said Jessica bravely. "I know nothing of the Gatekeepers *Mr Wicker*," she said, emphasising his name to show she knew who he was.

He turned on her in fury.

"Do not play gamesss with me little girl. I know you have them!" he shouted.

Then in a calmer voice he said, "My name is not Mr Wicker. Here I am known as Brain Drainer. But you and your friends will get to know me very well. Enough of this!" he shouted. "Take them to the Tiggler! But leave this one for me," he pointed to Rebecca. "Find the canine and kill him!"

James, Rebecca and Jessica were then separated and each thrown into long, narrow, box-like containers. Jessica was in total darkness and could only guess that they were being carried somewhere. She was absolutely terrified and all she could think of was Tom running, running and getting help.

It was not long before they came to a stop and Jessica was dropped roughly to the floor. She could just make out some muffled voices.

It sounded as though someone was giving a command, then silence. Jessica felt very cramped inside the box and the air was beginning to get stale. But it was almost preferable to stay there. She was terrified by the thought of what might happen when she was taken out. Then the lid of the box was removed and Jessica was harshly dragged out by an agent. She was thrown into a tiny, dark cell, which was cut out of rock and had no windows.

The agent slammed the door shut and growled through the bars, "I'll be back for you. You have a meeting with the Tiggler!"

Jessica didn't know what to do. There was nothing she could do. She tried to think of nice things. She closed her eyes and thought about all the things that made her happy. She tried to picture being rescued and the vile agents being defeated. Then she thought, for the first time since arriving in the Invisible World, of her parents. But the thought made her cry. She missed them terribly and would have given anything to be back home with them again.

Suddenly she remembered the dragonfly. *Oh no*, she thought, *what has happened to Ashley?* In the confusion she had totally forgotten about him. She felt terrible, but come to think of it, she could not recall having seen him with any of the agents.

Jessica's thoughts were interrupted by the return of her captor. He opened the door and said, "Come with me. There's someone who would like to meet you."

Jessica walked in front of the agent and every now and then he would prod her in the back to make her walk faster. They walked down a long, dimly lit corridor until they reached the end, where there was a door. The agent opened it and pushed Jessica inside. She found herself in a small room. In the middle of the room, there was what looked like a rusty old dentist chair with restraints attached to it. The agent made Jessica sit in the chair and roughly tied the restraints around her so that she could not move. Then he left the room. Jessica noticed that high up on the wall to her right was a small opening with bars across it. Jessica guessed that there was another room on the other side of the opening. Then it started.

Jessica could hear someone talking then the muffled sound of someone laughing, then screaming. She could not understand how someone could be laughing and screaming at the same time, but realised to her horror that it was James she could hear. The sound seemed to go on for a long time. Jessica was petrified and extremely disturbed by the fact that it was her friend making the noise. Then the sounds stopped. Moments later, the door to where Jessica was being held opened.

A very strange looking woman walked through and stood, looking at Jessica. The woman was young and not much taller than Jessica. Her red hair was scraped back from her face and pinned high up on her head and she was wearing dark glasses, even though it was not bright in the room. The skin on her face was very pale and her lips were bright red like her hair. She did not appear to have any ears, but instead, Jessica noticed that there were two tiny black antennae sticking out on either side of her head. She was dressed in a long, flowing black chiffon dress and her arms were completely covered by long, wide sleeves.

"I have been getting acquainted with your friend," the woman said. "He is very strong, it will take a long time to break him. But perhaps if you tell me what I want to know, he can be spared."

"Who, who are you?" asked Jessica, terrified.

The woman moved closer and leant in very near to Jessica. She whispered in her ear, "I am your worst nightmare."

Then she stood back and lifted her arms up in the air. As she did so, the sleeves of her dress fell down past her elbows to reveal eight disgusting arms. Each of the arms writhed with dozens of

eel, leech-like creatures that moved of their own accord, their mouths full of vicious teeth.

"I am the Tiggler!" the woman cried and shrieked with laughter. "I tickle my victims till they go insane or die. Your friend seems to enjoy my touch, as he is not willing to tell me what I want to know. Perhaps you will not be so difficult to break."

The woman took a step nearer to Jessica.

Just then, Jessica heard shouting coming from outside the room. The woman stopped and listened. Then they heard a dog barking. It was Tom!

Jessica was ecstatic and started to shout, "Tom! Tom! I'm in here, Tom!"

"You be silent!" shouted the woman to Jessica. "I'll be back for you," she added as she left the room.

It sounded like mayhem outside. Jessica could hear more shouting, Tom barking, shouting, a woman screaming, then nothing. Jessica struggled to try to get free from the restraints but it was no use. She would just have to sit tight and hope that someone would come for her.

She was just about to shout for Tom again when she noticed them coming towards her from under the doorway. Jessica was not sure, but she thought that the tiny black specks she could see before her were ants! Yes, they were ants! Before she knew what was happening, Jessica was surrounded by thousands of them. They were walking across the floor to get to her and when they began to climb up her legs she started to shout. What atrocity was she about to be subjected to? But then Jessica realised that the ants were actually unfastening her restraints. They were there to help!

Once the ants had freed Jessica, she got up and ran out of the door and almost knocked straight into someone.

"Porskin!" she cried. "You're here!"

"Yes," said Porskin, "Tom found me and brought me here. Thank the heavens you are alive."

"But James!" said Jessica. "They have James and they were torturing him Porskin and I couldn't help."

"Yes I know", said Porskin. "The ants will find him. Come we must leave."

With that they turned and ran back along the corridor. Then Jessica saw him. Thousands of ants had surrounded James and were carrying his body along the corridor.

"James!" cried Jessica. "Oh no, we're too late," she exclaimed at the sight of his limp body.

"He is alive," said Porskin, "barely, but he is alive."

They ran through the dungeon and it was then that Jessica noticed the lifeless bodies of several agents, including the Tiggler, on the floor.

"Up there," said Porskin pointing to an opening a short way ahead of them.

Then they heard Tom. He came bounding towards them and stood barking. He turned to run back the way he had come but stopped and stood barking at them.

"I think he wants us to follow him," said Jessica.

"Quickly then," said Porskin, "there may be others on their way."

They followed Tom back through the dungeon until they came to a set of stone stairs. Tom barked and ran up the stairs followed closely by Porskin and Jessica.

When they reached the top, they found themselves standing at the edge of what looked like an enormous pit. The pit was so deep that it was difficult for Jessica to see what was moving below. Then she realised. The pit was full of cats! There were hundreds of them and they were trapped.

"It's the cats!" yelled Jessica. "The ones the Shadow Beings are going to destroy!"

- CHAPTER TWELVE -

JAMES

"We must release the cats," said Porskin.

He looked over the edge of the pit and saw that there was a rope leading down to the bottom.

"Put your arms round my neck and hold on tight," he said to Jessica.

Jessica did as she was told and Porskin climbed down the rope with Jessica holding onto him. The sound of cats meowing was extremely loud and their smell intense. Jessica held her hand over her nose and mouth.

"Look, there," said Porskin pointing to what seemed to be an opening at the side of the pit.

They started to pick their way through the mass of cats to get to the doorway.

"Wait," said Jessica. "One of the Gatekeepers might be here. We should look before we release them."

"It could be any one of these," said Porskin, "how will you know which one to choose?"

Jessica looked at the hundreds of cats in front of her and thought it was a hopeless task.

Just then something caught her eye. In the middle of the pit, there was one cat in particular, a black cat with unusual blue eyes, it looked strangely familiar. It had caught Jessica's attention because it seemed to be playing. It was leaping in the air and chasing something. When Jessica took a closer look, she realised that the cat was chasing a butterfly!

"It's a sign," she said to Porskin. "It's a sign from Lily, I know it is."

Then Jessica thought she heard a voice very close to her say, "The locket. Check the locket."

"Of course!" shouted Jessica.

She took the locket from around her neck and opened it.

"I knew I recognised that cat," she said.

She held the locket up for Porskin to see.

"Look," she said, "it's the cat, the one my grandmother is holding in the photo. It's the same cat!"

"I'll get it," Porskin said and proceeded to wade through the feline throng.

Jessica looked at the photograph again. Then her attention turned to the picture on the left-hand side of the locket, the one of the little girl.

"Wait a minute," she said out loud to herself. "I know that girl. It's Rebecca!"

Jessica did not have time to consider what the picture of Rebecca might mean. Porskin grabbed the cat and shouted at Jessica to head for the door.

Porskin and Jessica ran through the doorway and into the sunlight outside. They were followed by a stream of cats of every size, shape and colour. They were soon joined by Tom and the ants who were carrying an unconscious James.

"We must take James somewhere secure," Porskin said. "More agents will be here soon."

They followed the ants who led them to an enormous, elongated structure. Jessica guessed that it was their home, their ant-hill.

The ant-hill was large enough for them all to fit inside. It was cramped but at least it was safe and away from the agents. Jessica and Porskin watched as the ants took care of James and nursed him. They made him as comfortable as possible and brought him water and a little food. Tom did not move from his side the whole time.

Jessica and Porskin waited patiently and after some time, James came around.

"Hello you," said Jessica softly to James, "how do you feel?"

"Oh, I've been better," croaked James. "Where are we?" he asked.

"We're with friends," said Jessica, "and Porskin is here and Tom."

James put his hand out to feel for his companion. Tom whined and licked James' hand.

"We have found another Gatekeeper," said Jessica.

James turned his head and looked at the black cat sitting beside her.

"Rebecca?" asked James. "Where is Rebecca?"

Jessica could not bear to answer his question.

"She has been taken," said Porskin. "The Brain Drainer has her."

James closed his eyes and quietly said, "Then we are already lost."

He tried to sit up. "I must, I must go to the future," he said.

"You are too weak now," said Porskin.

"I must," said James, "she is my sister. I must find out if she still lives and how we will fare in all this."

Porskin bowed his head low and said, "You must do what you think is right my friend."

James closed his eyes. Jessica looked at him intensely and right before her eyes, he began to age. His forehead became furrowed with frown lines and he moaned quietly as though he were in pain.

"James, James." Jessica whispered whilst shaking him gently.

James slowly opened his eyes and looked at her.

"The balance has swung," he said. It seemed to take great effort for him to speak. "The future is dark. I cannot see. Without Rebecca there is no hope. Without love there is no hope."

He coughed as though he were choking on the words.

"Is she still alive?" asked Porskin.

"Yes. Just," James said. Then he looked at Jessica. "You must, you must get to her," he said. "Without her there is no hope. We will all perish. You must, you m – ."

He passed away before he was able to finish the word.

"James. James," Jessica called.

But she knew he had gone.

Tom sat up, lifted his head and howled. The tears ran down Jessica's face. Porskin stood up, took one last look at James and left the ant-hill in silence. Jessica closed her eyes and sat very still.

After some time, she became aware of a very bright light penetrating her eyelids. She slowly opened her eyes and gasped. Tom was completely surrounded by a beautiful golden light and as she looked on, Jessica saw that Tom was changing form. He began to transform. His fur disappeared and his snout became shorter. His large ears vanished and he grew in size. Jessica was awestruck. When the metamorphosis was complete, sitting in front of her where Tom had once been, was an angel! His beautiful, dark skin was as black as ebony and he had the most loving, deep brown eyes. His wings were large and powerful and covered in the softest, downy feathers. He was breath taking.

Jessica could not speak. The angel lent over James' body and kissed him tenderly on the forehead. Then he put one of his hands to James' chest. A golden light emitted from his heart and went into James' body.

When he took his hand away, Jessica saw that he was holding the three cats. He turned to Jessica and said, "You must take the Gatekeepers now. It is up to you to continue the quest. Much relies upon your success."

With that he handed Jessica the cats and touched her cheek tenderly. She felt a warm glow enter her body.

"I must leave you now," said the angel. "I must take James home."

The angel effortlessly picked James' body up from the ground and in an instant, they were gone.

Jessica was dazed. She felt a mixture of sadness and great hope. She could still feel the warmth of the angel's touch and was comforted by the thought that Tom, James' guardian angel, had been with them all along. Jessica looked at the three cats in her hands. The black cat who was still sitting beside her nudged them with his nose and purred loudly. Just then, Jessica saw something out of the corner of her eye. Something was flying into the anthill. She couldn't believe it. It was Ashley!

The dragonfly flew straight to Jessica and landed softly on her head. Jessica giggled. She was delighted to see him.

"Ashley! How on earth did you know where to find me?" she asked. "And where have you been? I was so worried about you."

She instantly felt better now that he was there.

Jessica then gasped in surprise as Ashley began to speak.

"Jessica," Ashley said, "there is not much time and there are many things I must tell you."

"What did you say?" asked Jessica, unable to believe her ears. "Did you just speak? But h-how is it possible?" she stammered.

"Even after all you have seen, you still have trouble believing that anything is possible in the Invisible World!" Ashley said with a chuckle. "Do not be worried," he continued, "your innocence is one of the many special things about you. Now listen closely," he said, "for we must be on our way very soon. I am in hiding," began Ashley. "I could have taken many forms, but it seemed to me that no one would suspect a dragonfly" he laughed. "I also needed to be with you Jessica without my true identity being known. I know many, many things, particularly about the Gatekeepers and their role in the salvation of our worlds. The Shadow Beings have searched for me for a very long time and wish to use my knowledge of the Gatekeepers for their own malevolent purposes. I cannot allow that to happen. I have been able to evade capture up until now, but the Shadow Beings have grown strong and I fear that time is running out for me. That is why I must tell you what I know of the Gatekeepers. Then if anything should happen to me...As you know, there are five Gatekeepers in total and one Guardian. That is of course you Jessica. The Gatekeepers have taken the form of cats and each one has a special quality or magical power. The first represents Kindness. The second, Peace. These are the two cats your grandmother gave you Jessica. Next is Hope. That is the cat the merfolk gave you. Fourth is our friend Freedom whom I see is with us now."

He looked at the black cat sitting next to Jessica and continued. "And lastly Jessica, the most powerful of all the Gatekeepers is Love.

Without love the others cannot exist, as they all stem from love."

"And that is the one we do not have," said Jessica sadly.

"That is true," replied Ashley. "It is the responsibility of the Gatekeepers to keep all life in balance and to ensure the dark realm does not rule the planets as it once did. Without the Gatekeepers there will be rampant cruelty, rage, despair, slavery and hatred. But I'm afraid there is little time left Jessica and without the fifth cat—"

"We can still find the fifth cat, I know we can," said Jessica trying to sound positive.

Ashley shook his head. "Have you not realised yet?" he asked. "Rebecca is the fifth cat. She is the last Gatekeeper."

It finally hit Jessica. Of course! That is why her picture was in the locket and why Brain Drainer took her and why James seemed so desperate!

Jessica was stunned. She looked at Ashley with tears in her eyes and said, "What are we to do now? Is it hopeless Ashley, have we lost the battle?"

"There is always hope," replied Ashley, "for without it, the Shadow Beings have already triumphed."

"But what can be done?" implored Jessica.

"We must carry on," said Ashley, "we must find Rebecca and defeat the Shadow Beings. It is up to us now."

- CHAPTER FOURTEEN -

BRAIN DRAINER

Before Jessica and Ashley set off, they asked the black cat to return to inanimate form so that he could be hidden. The cat willingly obliged and instantly became a small, heavy ornament carved from smooth black wood. Jessica looked at him closely for a while and marvelled at his beautiful turquoise blue eyes. Then she carefully hid him from sight. Jessica and Ashley thanked the ants for their help and bade them farewell.

Jessica's heart was heavy and she felt weighed down by the enormity of the task ahead. But she was glad that Ashley was with her.

"Do you know where they may have taken Rebecca?" asked Jessica.

"Yes, I believe so," replied Ashley. "I'm sure that she has been taken to the Fortress. It is a terrible place Jessica. It will be very, very dangerous for us."

"What will they do to her?" asked Jessica.

Ashley's whole body seemed to quiver.

"It is better that you do not know," he replied.

The journey was hard and heavy going. The further they went the more desolate their surroundings became. Jessica was beginning to think that it really was too late. She felt as though they were in an awful nightmare and she shuddered at the thought that if they did not succeed, Earth and all the planets would become like this.

Just then, Jessica thought she saw a lone figure far away on the horizon ahead of them. It was gone again in an instant. It was the only thing that Jessica had seen in the miles of deserted wasteland.

"Hey," she said to Ashley, "did you see that?"

"Yes, I did," he replied.

"Do you think we should see who it is? Jessica asked.

Ashley did not answer for some time, then said, "It is your decision now. You must take us where you feel we need to go."

"Is there time?" Jessica asked, hoping to get some information from him.

Ashley did not answer. They continued to walk and Jessica spotted the figure again but it disappeared in moments.

"I think we should find out who that is," Jessica said, "they might be able to help us."

Jessica headed in the general direction of where she had seen the figure. *Where could they have gone*, she thought.

There was nowhere to hide and she was beginning to think her eyes were playing tricks on her, when she heard someone say, "Pssst, over here."

Jessica looked round and spotted a hand waving at her from out of the ground some distance away. Jessica went to investigate and realised that there was a small hole in the ground that had been camouflaged.

"Quickly," the voice said, "come down, come down."

Jessica took a second to decide, then she crouched down, looked into the hole and saw that there was a ladder. In moments she was on the ladder and climbing down a narrow shaft. Once she was at the bottom she saw that she was in a passageway. At the end of the passageway she saw a figure in the shadows.

"Come this way," said the person as they disappeared through a doorway.

Jessica followed the stranger and when she got to the door, she opened it and walked through.

Jessica looked around her. It was unbelievable. She was standing in the middle of what appeared to be an enormous library! Jessica had never seen so many books in one place before.

As Jessica looked round she became aware of a figure watching her. It was an elderly lady. She was not very tall and was dressed in amazing coloured silk robes. Her face looked very old and was covered in lines and wrinkles, but Jessica could tell that she must have been very beautiful once upon a time.

The thing that was most striking about the lady though was her hair. It was light brown in colour, which Jessica thought strange given her age, and it fell down the whole length of her body, almost to the floor. It was the longest hair Jessica had ever seen.

"Hello," Jessica ventured, "who are you?"

"I am the librarian," replied the old lady. "Welcome to the library of a trillion endings. Now my friend," she said, "there is not much time. Each of the books within this library contains a different ending to your story. I have been looking after them, waiting for you to come Jessica."

"How do you know my name?" asked Jessica with astonishment.

The old lady just smiled.

"The end is still unknown," the old lady continued, "it has not been decided yet, so there is still time. You must choose Jessica. You must choose one book from the library. That will be the ending to your story. Choose wisely."

Jessica looked around at the books.

"But how do I know which one to choose?" she asked in dismay. "There are so many, how do I know I've picked the right one?"

"Follow your heart," the old lady said. "Follow your heart. You will know which one to choose."

Jessica stood completely still for a moment. Then she looked around once more and walked towards a small cabinet she had seen in a corner of the library. Jessica opened the cabinet, took a deep breath and closed her eyes. As she ran her hands across the books she asked for help to choose the right one. Then her hand stopped on a book. She had felt drawn to it. Jessica opened her eyes and saw that she was touching a very small book, which had a plain brown, worn cover.

"Is that the one?" asked the old lady.

"I think so," replied Jessica, "but it is so small and plain."

"You may choose again," said the old lady.

Jessica closed her eyes and held the book close to her chest.

"No," she said, "this is the one."

"Then it is done," the old lady said. "The end has been decided. Now we must wait to see what happens."

She turned and slowly walked away.

"Wait!" called Jessica. "I know you, don't I," she said.

The old lady turned to face Jessica and said, "Of course my old friend. I am you."

With that, she walked through an archway of books and was gone.

"Jessica," Ashley said gently, "it is time we were on our way."

Jessica nodded. She wanted to stay and ask the lady, her older self, more questions. But she knew they had to go. The pair made their way back through the library, along the passageway and up the ladder.

Jessica and Ashley continued their journey. Before long they came to the edge of a river. The water was black and stinking. In the distance, on the other side they could see a huge ominous looking black tower. It was the Fortress. Ashley flew to the other side of the river whilst Jessica walked along the bank looking for a section that was narrow enough to cross. Jessica walked back a few paces, then ran towards the edge and leapt across. She did not want to fall in the foul-smelling water. Once she was across, they headed for the Fortress.

The nearer Jessica and Ashley got, the larger

and more sinister the black tower seemed to become. It loomed over them like an enormous, monstrous, twisted black tree. Jessica shuddered. She was beginning to feel ill-equipped for facing what might be inside.

Then, as if it knew they were there, the heavy iron door of the Fortress opened with an eerie creak. Jessica stepped inside and jumped when the iron door closed with a loud bang behind them. The sound echoed through the stone walls. Jessica slowly crept forward, expecting to be confronted by agents of the Shadow Beings at any moment. But they were alone.

"Which way should we go?" asked Jessica.

"How about there, look," Ashley said as he nodded towards a spiral staircase he had seen on their left. As Jessica approached the staircase she could feel all the hairs on the back of her neck rise. She could almost feel the wickedness of the place oozing out of the stone and creeping towards them. She was not feeling at all brave, but the thought of what might be happening to Rebecca pushed her on.

As they began to climb the stairs, Jessica could hear noises coming from above them. As they reached the next level of the Fortress, Jessica realised that the sounds were coming from a corridor to her right. As she approached the corridor she noticed that set into the walls, were rows upon rows of dark, filthy cells. That was where the noises were coming from. The Fortress was so dark that she was finding it difficult to see clearly.

As she moved nearer to one of the cells, a hand shot out through the bars and grabbed her! Jessica screamed.

"It's alright," whispered a voice, "I'm not going to hurt you."

Jessica's heart was beating fast.

"Who, who are you?" she said.

"We have been captured by the Shadow Beings," said the voice, "and are being held prisoner here. Have you come to free us?"

As Jessica's eyes adjusted to the gloom she could see that the voice belonged to a dwarf. As she peered into the cell, she saw that he was surrounded by at least forty or so other prisoners. Some Jessica recognised as elves, fairies, leprechauns and fauns, and some Jessica could not put a name to.

"Oh, you poor things," said Jessica sadly. "I will try to free you but I must find my friend. I don't have much time."

"Are you looking for the beautiful girl with golden hair?" asked one of the fairies.

"Yes, have you seen her?" asked Jessica.

"Brain Drainer has her," replied the fairy. "I think he has taken her to the top of the tower."

"I will stay here," said Ashley, "and try to free them. Go! You must get to Rebecca."

Jessica left Ashley and ran back to the spiral staircase where she made her way up higher and higher to the top of the tower. Jessica slowly crept up the last few steps. At the top she could see two figures. One, a girl, who was strapped to a chair; the other, a large, dark figure who was leaning over her. Jessica gasped as she realised it was Rebecca and leaning over her was Brain Drainer! But he looked different.

Jessica no longer recognised him as Mr Wicker. His entire head and part of his body, down to his knees, was encased in what looked like a large black cone. The cone was segmented like the body of a cockroach and the top of the cone ended in a long, thin snout. Jessica could see that on either side of the cone were enlarged blue eyes, as though a magnifying glass were being held in front of them. Coming out of the end of the snout were two, thin probes that looked like white worms. Jessica recoiled in horror when she realised that the two worm probes were attached to Rebecca through her nose! Rebecca was extremely pale and her eyes were rolling in her head. It looked as though her very life force was being sucked from her.

"Stop! Stop!" screamed Jessica. "You're killing her. Stop!"

Without thinking she ran towards Brain Drainer and began to beat him on the back with her clenched fists. He turned around in surprise and the two probes were pulled from Rebecca's nose. She slumped forwards in the chair.

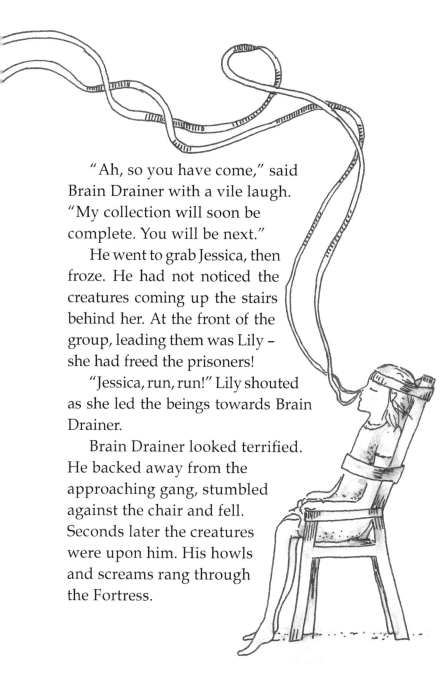

"Ah, so you have come," said
Brain Drainer with a vile laugh.
"My collection will soon be
complete. You will be next."

He went to grab Jessica, then
froze. He had not noticed the
creatures coming up the stairs
behind her. At the front of the
group, leading them was Lily –
she had freed the prisoners!

"Jessica, run, run!" Lily shouted
as she led the beings towards Brain
Drainer.

Brain Drainer looked terrified.
He backed away from the
approaching gang, stumbled
against the chair and fell.
Seconds later the creatures
were upon him. His howls
and screams rang through
the Fortress.

"Lily, thank goodness you're here!" cried Jessica as she ran to her grandmother.

But her relief was short lived. At that moment they all stopped and listened.

It started as a distant drone then grew louder and louder. Before they knew what was happening, the roof of the tower was being ripped apart, and there, hovering above them were the Shadow Beings! The sound they had heard became a deafening buzz. Jessica realised that the Shadow Beings were made up of millions upon millions of mosquito-type creatures. She put her hands over her ears, but it was no use. The sound penetrated her skull, she cried out in pain. Then the shape of the Shadow Beings changed and seemed to form an enormous, giant hand. Moments later the hand shot through the hole in the roof and grabbed Rebecca, ripping her out of the chair. In seconds the Shadow Beings and Rebecca were gone. There was silence.

- CHAPTER FIFTEEN -

THE SHADOW BEINGS

"We have to go after them!" shouted Lily to Jessica.

"Where is Ashley?" cried Jessica.

"I've not seen anyone else," replied Lily. "I just knew I had to release the prisoners and that you were in trouble. Come on, we have to go!"

With that she grabbed Jessica by the hand and the two fled back down the spiral staircase, followed closely by the beings Lily had released.

Once outside they ran and ran. In the distance they could just make out the dark mass of Shadow Beings in the sky. They looked enormous even from far away.

Just when Jessica thought she could not run anymore, two horses trotted up beside them and shouted, "Let us carry you, it will be much quicker."

Jessica and Lily gratefully climbed onto the horses' backs and they ran like the wind. Up ahead of them, Jessica could see a huge rock jutting out of the ground, rising high into the sky above. As they drew nearer, she could see that there were stone steps carved into the rock, which led to the top of its flat summit. In the middle of the summit, Jessica thought she could see what looked like a large stone and there appeared to be someone tied to it. Jessica could also see that the rock was completely surrounded by thousands of agents of the Shadow Beings.

Jessica and Lily reached the bottom of the monolith, dismounted from the horses and went to step onto the rock. They were pushed back by an invisible force field and were thrown to the ground a few feet away. The sky above them became dark. Jessica looked up and could see the swirling, buzzing Shadow Beings above them. They had almost entirely blocked out the light from the sun. Then they heard the booming voices.

"GIVE THE GATEKEEPERS TO US," said the voices.

The ground below them shook.

"No!" shouted Jessica, but her voice sounded tiny and insignificant.

"GIVE THEM TO US OR YOU WILL ALL PERISH!" said the voices. "WE HAVE THE GIRL NOW. IT IS NO USE. GIVE IN TO OUR WILL AND YOU WILL BE SPARED."

"NO!" shouted Jessica again.

Then she took a deep breath and called out, "Rebecca! Rebecca! Remember who you are! You are the last Gatekeeper! Please Rebecca, remember who you ARRRE!"

Jessica then took the four cats she had been hiding and placed them gently on the ground in front of her. She closed her eyes tightly, and as she did so, she recited the poem Lily had given to her.

> *"So five there are*
> *And five there'll be,*
> *I have travelled far*
> *So come with me.*
> *Come wise cats, hear my call,*
> *The forever darkness must never fall.*
> *Come sing with me and our hearts will soar,*
> *The dark realm will hide when it hears your roar."*

Jessica opened her eyes slowly. The earth started to shake as though an almighty earthquake were erupting beneath them. Then the cats began to change. First, they became real cats once more, then they grew in size. As Jessica looked on in amazement she realised that one by one the cats were changing into their true form.

The grey cat became a huge jaguar and as she roared she said, "*I am Kindness!*"

The golden cat became a powerful lion and as he roared he said, "*I am Peace!*"

The shell cat became an elegant cheetah and she said, "*I am Hope!*"

Finally, the black cat became a panther and as he roared he said, "*I am Freedom!*"

"Where is Love?" cried Jessica, looking up at the rock in desperation.

"I am here!" called Rebecca.

She had broken free of her bonds and as she ran down the stone steps towards Jessica, she turned into the most beautiful white tiger.

As she stood next to Jessica she cried, "*I am Love!*"

She lifted her head and roared. At that moment, the diamond in Jessica's locket was activated, and it emitted a magnificent beam of pure white light which completely surrounded them.

"NO! NO! NO!" thundered the Shadow Beings as the white light shone up the side of the rock towards them.

As the light reached the Shadow Beings, the two forces, light and dark were locked together in battle. Whilst the Light and the Shadow Beings fought, the Gatekeepers, with the help of the others, battled with the agents of the Shadows Beings.

As the battle continued, Jessica noticed a brilliant white horse approaching. As she looked she realised that it was in fact a unicorn! And walking behind the unicorn were hundreds of beautiful angels. Jessica also saw, that riding on the unicorn's back was a dragonfly. It was Ashley!

"Ashley!" she called. "Ashley! We're winning. We are winning Ashley!"

Ashley did not respond. As he got closer to Jessica, a flash of light surrounded him and as she looked, Jessica could just make out that he was changing form. The light was so bright that Jessica had to shield her eyes and could no longer see Ashley.

As the light began to fade and Jessica was able to look once more, she realised that Ashley had disappeared and, in his place, sat a person who was wearing a cloak and a cover over his face.

"Porskin? Porskin is that you?" Jessica asked with delight and confusion.

"Yes, it is Porskin," replied the man.

"But, but Ashley, what has happened to Ashley?"

"We are one and the same he and I," answered Porskin and with that he threw off his cloak and head covering.

A collective gasp went around, then silence fell upon all of them.

Jessica heard someone shout, "The One. It is! It is the One!"

Others joined in and before long hundreds of voices were shouting, "The One! The One!"

As Jessica watched in awe, Porskin became a beautiful light being. She could no longer make out his features for his whole body was bursting with rays of golden white light and he was surrounded by dozens of tiny rainbows.

The One dismounted from the unicorn and walked towards Jessica. She was speechless.

"Jessica," he said; his voice was rich and wondrous. "As the Guardian, it is up to you to decide the fate of the Shadow Beings. You may choose if they live or if they die."

"But, but I-I cannot decide that," stammered Jessica.

"Look inside your heart," said the One, "and tell me what choice you will make. But remember Jessica. Every being has the ability to reflect the light, but every one of us casts a shadow."

Jessica closed her eyes and searched her heart.

Then she looked at the One and said, "Have pity on the Shadow Beings. We must choose the way of kindness, peace, hope, freedom and love. Above all, love."

"So be it," said the One. "You have chosen wisely Jessica."

With that he turned to face the rock and, as he did so, he held his arms open and said, "Come my children. Come home where you belong. You have much still to learn."

The One opened his mouth and drew in a long, deep breath. As he did so, the Shadow Beings and all their followers were taken inside the One and could no longer be seen.

"You may live in peace again!" cried the One.

A cheer went up all around them. Then the One looked at Jessica once more.

"Thank you little one. You have shown great courage, wisdom, kindness and compassion. You have demonstrated that humans are still worthy of the guardianship of the Gatekeepers. May it long continue! Now Jessica, to thank you for what you have done, I may grant you one request. What is it to be?"

Jessica looked up at the One and simply said, "I wish to go home."

- CHAPTER SIXTEEN -

FIVE CAT MAGIC

Jessica slowly opened her eyes. Then she yawned and stretched. As she turned her head she saw that her parents were sitting beside her. They were asleep.

"Mum, Dad." Jessica called softly.

Her mother opened her eyes and blinked. When she saw that Jessica was awake she leapt out of her chair and began kissing Jessica all over her face.

"Oh, Jess, Jess!" she was saying.

"Mike, Mike, wake up! It's Jessica, she's awake, she's ok, she's awake!"

Jessica's father stood up and gave his daughter a huge hug.

"Jess, Jess," he said, "you're really awake! Thank the heavens, thank the angels."

Jessica was puzzled.

"What's going on guys?" she asked. "Why are you acting so strangely? And where am I?"

As Jessica took in her surroundings, she realised that she was lying in bed and that she was in a hospital.

"What's going on?" she asked again. "What am I doing here?"

"Oh Jess," said her mother, "it was awful. You had a terrible accident. Don't you remember? That day you were walking to school, you went to cross the road and, and—" Her mother started to cry.

"And a car hit you," continued her father. He took a deep breath before he carried on. "And the thing is Jess, that was almost eight months ago. You've been asleep in a coma ever since."

The doctors and nurses made a huge fuss of Jessica over the next few days. They could not believe how well she was doing and what a remarkable recovery she was making. Jessica was still a bit dazed. An accident? A coma? She couldn't take it all in. So what about everything else? The cats, Porskin, the One, the Shadow Beings. Had it all been a strange dream? Had her mind just been making it up whilst she was asleep? She didn't know. And now that she was back in the *real world* she was even less certain.

"Jess," Mum said one day. "The doctors say you should be able to go home soon, so there is something I need to tell you." She paused. "The thing is, you have a baby brother."

"What?" asked Jessica in amazement. "What do you mean? Why didn't you tell me before?"

"I didn't want to bombard you," said Mum. "I was only a couple of months pregnant when you had the accident and he was born a few weeks ago."

"That's fantastic Mum," Jessica said. "What's he called?"

"Your Dad and I haven't decided on a name yet," said Mum. "We were hoping that maybe you would choose one for him."

"Well," said Jessica, "I shall have to meet him first."

The next day Mum brought Jessica's baby brother to the hospital so she could meet him for the first time. It was love at first sight for them both. Jessica thought he was gorgeous.

"Will you help me change his nappy please?" asked Mum.

"Of course," said Jessica, "but you'll have to show me how."

As Jessica helped her Mum undress the small baby, she noticed something on his chest.

"What's that?" she asked Mum pointing to it.

"Oh that," said Mum. "I think it's a birthmark or something."

Jessica took a closer look and sure enough, it was a tiny birthmark in the middle of his chest in the shape of what looked like a lock!

"James?" said Jessica in disbelief.

"That's a lovely name," said Mum. "Shall we call him James? Yes, I think he looks like a James." The baby waved his arms. "I think he likes it too."

Jessica was discharged from the hospital and was thankful to be home. The family were busy getting things ready for baby James' naming ceremony and party and Jessica was getting stronger and stronger by the day. Then before long, it was the night before James' special day. Jessica went to bed early as she always did the night before something exciting, as it seemed to make the morning come around more quickly. She kissed both her parents goodnight, gave baby James a big hug and went off to bed.

As she drifted off to sleep that night, Jessica thought of Lily and of all the wonderful people she had met in the Invisible World. She did not know if they had been real or not, but she would treasure the memory of them forever. Jessica slept deeply that evening and had wonderful dreams. The next morning it was time for the naming ceremony and Jessica was very excited. As she jumped out of bed she noticed a beautifully wrapped parcel on the floor. There was a small envelope with a card inside which read,

Dearest Jessica. My brave girl. Guard them well.
With all my love
L xxx

Jessica gasped. Could it be, could it really be? She hurriedly opened the parcel and inside she found a magnificent wooden box with a tiny silver key sticking out of the lock. She opened the box and looked inside. To her delight there were five beautiful cat ornaments. She touched them reverently and picked one up. It was a lovely white cat made from mother of pearl and it had the most beautiful rose quartz crystal eyes. Jessica planted a kiss on the cat's head and said, "Rebecca."

Then she noticed another smaller package hiding underneath the torn wrapping. Jessica carefully unwrapped it and held the gift in her hands, looking at it for some time. It was a very small book with a plain brown, worn cover. Jessica looked at the title and read out loud. It simply said, "Chapter 13."